THE HEIRESS'S
SECRET BABY

THE HEIRESS'S SECRET BABY

BY

JESSICA GILMORE

First published in Great Britain 2015
by Mills & Boon, an imprint of Harlequin (UK) Limited,
Large Print edition 2015
Eton House, 18-24 Paradise Road,
Richmond, Surrey, TW9 1SR

ISBN: 978-0-263-25645-1

Harlequin (UK) Limited's policy is to use papers that are natural, renewable and recyclable products and made from wood grown in sustainable forests. The logging and manufacturing processes conform to the legal environmental regulations of the country of origin.

Printed and bound in Great Britain
by CPI Antony Rowe, Chippenham, Wiltshire

For Jo M

It seems pretty fitting that a book with a Parisian setting is dedicated to you just as we plan our girls' trip to Paris! I'm not sure how you have managed to be so positive and supportive and brilliant during the past five years; I am completely in awe of your strength. Thank you so much for being such a fantastic friend to me and an inspiration (and ever-patient hairstylist) to Abs.

Here's to Paris and most of all to medical advances and to a happy, healthy future xxx

CHAPTER ONE

My Secret Bucket List

~~Swim in the sea, naked~~
~~NB: in azure warm seas, not in the North Sea~~
~~Sleep out under the stars~~
~~Have sex on the beach~~
~~NB: the real deal, not the cocktail~~
~~Drink an authentic margarita~~
Fall in love in Paris

POLLY READ THE list through for the last time, feeling the carefree *joie de vivre* fall away and the old, familiar cloaks of respectability and responsibility settling back onto her shoulders. They were a little heavy, but maybe that was to be expected after three months away.

Three months, five wishes. And she'd achieved four out of the five, which wasn't bad going. The heaviness lifted for a second as the highlights of the last three months flashed through her mind and then it descended again.

What had she been thinking? She might as well have written the list in a silver pen and decorated it with pink love hearts and butterflies, pinning it on her wall next to a lipstick-kiss-covered poster of a pre-pubescent boy band.

Polly pulled the page out of her diary and, without allowing herself a second's pause to reconsider, tore it into pieces. It was time to reposition her three-month sabbatical into something more appropriate for the new CEO of a company with a multimillion-pound turnover.

She chewed on the end of her pen for a moment and then started a new list.

My Bucket List

~~Travel to the Galapagos Islands~~
See the Northern Lights
~~Walk the Inca Trail~~
Write a book
See tigers in the wild

There, two achieved, three to aspire to and all perfectly respectable. Not a grain of sand in any place it definitely shouldn't be...

The large luxurious town car drew to a smooth halt and jolted her back into the present day, away from dangerous memories. 'We're here, Miss Rafferty. Are you sure you don't want me to take you home first?'

Polly looked up from her diary and drew in a breath at the sight of the massive golden stone building stretching all the way down the block. She *was* home. Back at the famous department store founded by her great-grandfather. She hadn't expected to ever see it again, let alone to walk in as mistress of all that she surveyed.

She stared at the huge picture windows flanking the iconic marble steps, her heart swelling with a potent mixture of love and pride. Each window told a tale and sold a dream. Rafferty's could give you anything, make you anyone—if you had the money to pay for it.

'This will be fine, Petyr, thank you. But please arrange for my bags to be taken back to Hopeford and for the concierge service to collect and launder them.'

She didn't want to set foot in Rafferty's carrying her rucksack stuffed as it was with sarongs, bikinis and walking boots, no matter how prestigious the brand names on them. Polly had spent a productive night at a hotel in Miami turning herself back into Miss Polly Rafferty from Miss Carefree Backpacker—all it had taken was a little shopping, a manicure and a wash and blow-dry.

She was back and she was ready.

Petyr opened the car door for her and Polly slid out onto the pavement, breathing in deeply as she did so. Car fumes, perfume, hot concrete, fried food—London in the height of summer. How she'd missed it. She pulled down her skirt hem and wriggled her toes experimentally. The heels felt a little constrictive after three months of bare feet, flip-flops and walking boots but her feet would adjust back. She would adjust back. After all, this was her real dream; her time out had been nothing but a diversion along the way.

Polly lifted her new workbag onto her shoulder and headed straight for the main entrance. She was going in.

'Hello, Rachel.'

Oh, it had felt good walking through the hallowed halls, greeting the staff she knew by name and seeing the new ones jump as they realised just who was casting a quick, appraising eye over them. Good to see gossiping staff spring apart and how everyone suddenly seemed to find work to do.

Good that nobody dared to catch her eye. There must have been talk after her abrupt disappearance but it didn't seem to have affected her standing. She allowed herself a small sigh of relief.

But it was also good to go in through the Staff Only door, to be buzzed in by old Alf and see the welcome on his face. Alf had worked for Rafferty's since before Polly's father was born and had always had a bar of chocolate and a kind word for the small girl desperately trailing after her grandfather, wanting, *needing*, to be included.

And it was good to be here, back in the light-filled foyer where her assistant had her desk. Not that Rachel seemed to share her enthusiasm judging by her open-mouthed expression and panicked eyes, and the way her fingers shook as she gathered together a sheaf of papers.

'Miss Rafferty? We weren't expecting you back just yet.'

'I did let you know my flight details,' Polly said coolly. It wasn't like Rachel to be so disorganised.

And at the very least a friendly 'welcome back' would have been polite.

Rachel threw an anxious glance towards the door to Polly's office. 'Well yes.' She got up out of her chair and walked around her desk to stand in front of the door, blocking Polly's path. 'But I thought you would go home first. I didn't expect to see you today.'

'I hope my early appearance isn't too much of an inconvenience.' What was the girl hiding? Perhaps Raff had decorated her office in high gloss and black leather during his brief sojourn as CEO. 'As you can see I decided to come straight here.' Polly gave her assistant a cool glance, waiting for her to move aside.

'You've come straight from the airport?' Rachel wouldn't—or couldn't—meet her eye but stood her ground. 'You must be tired and thirsty. Why don't you go to the staff canteen and I'll arrange for them to bring you coffee and something to eat?'

'Coffee does sound lovely,' Polly agreed. 'But I'd rather have it *in* my office if you don't mind. Please call and arrange it. Thank you, Rachel.'

Rachel stood there for a long second, indecision

clear on her face before she moved slowly to one side. 'Yes, Miss Rafferty.'

Polly nodded curtly at her still-hovering assistant. Things had obviously got slack under Raff's reign. She hoped it wouldn't take too long to get things back on track—or to get herself back on track; no more lie-ins, long walks on beaches where the sand was so fine it felt like silk underfoot, no more swimming in balmy seas or drinking rum cocktails under the light of so many stars it was like being in an alternate universe.

No. She was back to work, routine and normality, which was great. A girl couldn't relax for ever, right?

Slowly Polly turned the chrome handle and opened her office door, relishing the cool polished feel of the metal under her hand. Like much of the interior throughout the store the door handle was one of the original art deco fittings chosen by her great-grandfather back in the nineteen twenties. His legacy lived on in every fitting and fixture. She loved the weight of history that fell onto her shoulders as soon as she walked into the building. Her name, her blood, her legacy.

She stood on the threshold for a second and

breathed in. It was finally hers. Everything she had worked for, everything she had dreamed of—this was her office, her store, her way.

And yet it had all felt so unachievable just three months ago. Despite four years as vice CEO and the last of those years as acting CEO while her grandfather stood back from the company he loved as fiercely as Polly herself did, she had walked away. After her grandfather had told her he was finally stepping down and installing Polly's twin brother Raff in his place she had dropped her swipe card on the desk, collected her bag and walked out.

The next day she had been on a plane to South America. She had left her home, her cat and her company—and replaced them with a frivolous bucket list.

Three months later that memory still had the power to wind her.

But here she was, back at the helm and nothing and no one was going to stand in her way.

The relief at seeing her office unchanged swept over her; the sunshine streaming in through the stained-glass floor-to-ceiling windows high-lighting the wood panelling, tiled floors and her beautiful walnut desk—the very same one commissioned by her great-grandfather for this room in nineteen twenty-five—the bookshelves and photos, her chaise longue, her...

Hang on. Her eyes skittered back; that hadn't been there before.

Or rather *he* hadn't.

Nope, Polly was pretty sure she would have remembered if she'd left a half-naked sleeping beauty on her antique chaise longue when she'd stormed out.

Frankly, the mood she'd been in, she probably would have taken him with her.

She moved a little closer, uncomfortably aware of her heels tapping on the tiled floor, and contemplated the newest addition to her office.

He was lying on his front, his arm pillowing his head, just the curve of a sharply defined cheekbone and a shock of dark hair falling over his forehead visible. His jeans were snug, low, riding deep on his back exposing every vertebrae on his naked torso.

It was a tanned torso, a deep olive, and although slim, almost to the point of leanness, every muscle was clearly defined. On his lower back a tree blossomed, a silhouette whose branches reached up to his middle vertebrae. Polly fought an urge to reach out and trace one of the narrow lines with her fingers. She didn't normally like tattoos but this one was oddly beautiful, almost mesmerising in its intricacy.

What was she doing? She shouldn't be standing here admiring the interloper. He needed to wake up and get out. No matter how peaceful he looked.

Polly coughed, a short, polite noise. It was as effectual as an umbrella in a hurricane. She coughed again, louder, more irritated.

He didn't even stir.

'Excuse me.' Her voice was soft, polite. Polly shook her head in disgust; this was her office. Why was *she* the one pussyfooting around? 'Excuse me!'

This time there was some effect, just a little; a faint murmur and a shift in his position as he rolled onto his side. She couldn't help flickering a quick glance along the lean length. Yep, the front matched the back, a smattering of fine dark hair tangled on his upper chest, another silky patch emphasising the muscles on his abdomen before tapering into a line that ran down inside the low-slung jeans.

Polly swallowed, her mouth suddenly in need of some kind of moisture. No, she scolded herself, tearing her eyes away, heat flushing through her. Just because he was in her office she didn't have the right to stand here and objectify him. She gave the room a quick once-over relieved that no one was there to witness her behaviour; she was the CEO for goodness' sake, she had to set an example.

This had gone on long enough. This was a place of business, not a doss house for disreputable if attractive young men to slumber in, or a hidey-hole for her PA's latest boyfriend. Whoever he was she was going to have to shake him awake. Right *now*.

If only he were wearing a shirt. Or anything. Touching that bronzed skin felt intrusive, intimate.

'For goodness' sake, are you woman or wombat?' she muttered, balling her fingers into a fist.

'Hello.' She reached over and took a tentative hold of one firm shoulder, his skin warm and smooth against her hand. 'Wake up.' She gave a little shake but it was like shaking a statue.

All she wanted was to sit at her desk and start working. Alone. Was that too much to ask? Anger and adrenaline flooded through her system; it had been a long journey, she was jet-lagged and irritated and in need of a sit-down and a coffee. She'd had enough. Officially.

Polly turned and walked crisply towards her small en-suite cloakroom and bathroom, this time uncaring of the loud tap of her heels. The door swung open to reveal a wide, airy space with room for coats and shoes plus a walk-in wardrobe where Polly stored a selection of outfits for the frequent occasions where she went straight from work to a social function. She gave the room a quick glance, relieved to see no trace of Raff's presence. It was as if he had been wiped out of the store's memory.

That was fine by her. He had made it quite clear he wanted nothing to do with Rafferty's—and although they were twins they had never been good at sharing.

Another door led into the well-equipped bathroom. Polly allowed herself one longing glance at the walk-in shower before grabbing a glass from the shelf and filling it with water, making sure the cold tap ran for a few seconds first for maximum chill. Then, quickly so that she didn't lose her nerve, she swivelled on her heel and marched back over to the chaise longue, standing over the interloper.

He had moved again, lying supine, half on his back, half on his side revealing more of his features. Long, thick lashes lay peacefully on cheekbones so finely sculpted it looked as if a master stonemason had been at work, eyebrows arching arrogantly above.

His wide mouth was slightly parted. Sensual, a little voice whispered to Polly. A mouth made for sin.

She ignored the voice. And she ignored the slight jibe of her conscience; she needed him awake and leaving; if he wouldn't respond to gentler methods then what choice did she have?

Resolutely Polly held the glass up over the man's face and tipped it. For one long moment she held it still so that the water was perfectly balanced right at the rim, clear drops so very close to spilling over the thin edge.

And then she allowed her hand to move the glass over the tipping point, a perfect stream of cold water falling like rain onto the peacefully slumbering face below.

Polly didn't quite know what to expect; anger, shock, contrition or even no reaction at all. He was so very deeply asleep after all. But what she didn't expect was for one red-rimmed eye to lazily open, for a smile to play around the disturbingly well-cut mouth or for a hand to shoot out and grab her wrist.

Caught by surprise, she stumbled forward, falling against the chaise as the hand snuck around her waist, pulling her down, pulling her close.

'Bonjour, chérie.' His voice was low, gravelly with sleep and deeply, unmistakeably French. 'If you wanted me to wake up you only had to ask.'

It was the shock, that was all. Otherwise she would have moved, called for help, disentangled herself from the strong arm anchoring her firmly against the bare chest. And she would never, *ever* have allowed his other hand to slip around her neck in an oddly sweet caress while he angled his mouth towards hers—would have moved away long before the hard mouth claimed hers in a distinctly unsleepy way.

It was definitely the shock keeping her paralysed under his touch—and she was definitely *not* leaning into the kiss, opening herself up to the pressure of his mouth on hers, the touch of his hand moving up her back, slipping round her ribcage, brushing against the swell of her breast.

Hang on, his hand was where?

Polly pulled away, jumping up off the chaise, resisting the urge to scrub the kiss off her tingling mouth.

Or to lean back down and let him claim her again.

'What do you think you're doing?'

'Saying *au revoir* of course.' He had shifted position and was leaning against the back of the chaise, his eyes skimming every inch of her until she wanted to wrap her arms around her torso, shielding herself from his insolent gaze.

'Au revoir?' Was she going mad? Where were the panicked apologies and the scuttling out of her office?

'Of course.' He raised an eyebrow. 'As you are dressed to leave I thought you were saying goodbye. But if it was more of a good morning...' the smile widened '...even better.'

'I am not saying *au revoir* or good morning or

anything but *what on earth are you doing in my office and where are your clothes*?'

She hadn't meant to tag on the last line but with the imprint of his hand still burning her back and the taste of him taunting her mouth she really needed to be looking at something other than what seemed like acres of taut, tanned bare flesh.

Surely now, now he would show some contrition, some shame. But no, he was what? Laughing? He was mad or drunk or both and she was going to call Security right now.

'Of course, your office! Polly, *bonjour.* I am charmed to meet you.'

What? He knew her name? She took an instinctive step backwards as he slid off the chaise, as graceful as a panther, and took a step towards her, hand held out.

'Who are you and what are you doing here?' She stepped back a little further, one hand groping for the phone ready to call for help.

'I am so very sorry.' He was smiling as if the whole situation were nothing but a huge joke. 'I fell asleep here, last night, and was confused when you woke me.' His eyes laughed at her, shamelessly. 'It's not the first time I've been awakened by a glass of water. I am Gabriel Beaufils, your new vice CEO. My friends call me Gabe. I hope you will too.'

No, that was no better, she was still looking at him as if he were an escaped convict. Not surprisingly, Gabe thought ruefully. What had he been thinking?

He hadn't. He'd been dreaming, stuck in that hazy world between sleep and wakefulness when he'd felt a warm hand on his shoulder followed by the chill shock of the water and, confused, had thought it some kind of game. After three weeks of eighteen-hour days, making sure he was fully and firmly ensconced at Rafferty's before the formidable Polly Rafferty returned, he wasn't as switched on as he should be.

Well, his wake-up call had been brutal. It was bad enough from Polly's point of view that he had been catapulted in without her say-so or knowledge—and a wake-up kiss probably wasn't the wisest way to make a good impression. He needed to make up the lost ground, and fast.

He smiled at her, pouring as much winning charm into the smile as he could.

There was no answering smile, not even in her

darkly shadowed eyes. The bruised circles were the only hint of tiredness even though she must have come straight here from the airport. Her dark gold hair was twisted up into a neat knot and her suit looked freshly laundered. Yet for all the business-style armour there was something oddly vulnerable in the blue eyes, the determined set of her almost too-slender frame.

'Gabriel Beaufils?' There was a hint of recognition in her voice. 'You were working for Desmoulins?'

'*Oui*, as Digital Director.' He debated mentioning the tripling of profits in the proud old Parisian store's web business but decided against it. Yet. That little but pertinent detail might come in handy and he didn't want to play his hand too soon.

'I don't recall hiring a new vice CEO.' There was nothing fragile in her voice. It was cold enough to freeze the water still dripping over his torso. 'Even if I had, that doesn't explain why you were sleeping in my office and appear to have mislaid your top.'

Nor why you kissed me. She might not have said

the words but they were implied, hung accusingly in the air.

No, better to forget about the kiss, delightful as it had been. Strange to think that the huge-eyed, fragile-looking woman opposite had responded so openly, so ardently, that she would taste of sweetness and spice.

Damn it, he was supposed to be forgetting about the kiss.

'Polly, *je suis désolé.*' This situation was not irredeemable no matter how it seemed right now. It wasn't often that Gabe thought himself lucky to have three older sisters but right now they were a blessing; he was used to disapproving glares and turning the stickiest of situations right around.

'I have been using this office until you returned—we didn't know if you would want to take over your grandfather's office or stay in here. But once again I was working too late and missed the last train back to Hopeford. It was easier to crash out on the couch rather than find a hotel so late. If I had known you were coming in this morning...'

He threw his hands out in a placatory gesture.

It didn't work. If anything she looked even more

suspicious. 'Hopeford? Why would you be staying there?'

A sinking feeling hit Gabe. On a scale of one to ten this whole situation was hitting one hundred on the awkward chart. If she wasn't happy about having a vice CEO she hadn't handpicked then she was going to love having a strange houseguest!

'Cat-feeding. Raff was worried Mr Simpkins would get lonely.' He smiled as winningly as he could but there was no response from her.

Okay, charm wasn't working, businesslike might. 'I do have an apartment arranged,' he explained. 'But unfortunately, just before I was going to move in, the neighbour's basement extension caused a massive subsidence in the whole street. I can quite easily go to a hotel if it's a problem but as your house was empty and I was homeless…' He shrugged. It had made perfect sense at the time.

Apparently not to Polly. 'You're staying in my *house*? Where is Raff? Why isn't he there?'

'He was in Jordan, now I think he's in Australia but he should be back soon.' It had been hard to keep up with the other Rafferty twin's travels.

'Australia? What on earth is he doing there?'

She sank down into the large chair behind her desk with an audible sigh of relief, probably worn out by the weight of all the questions she had fired at him. Gabe's head was spinning from them all.

'I thought Raff would wait until I got back before taking off again,' Polly murmured, her voice so low that Gabe hardly caught her words.

If Gabriel had to narrow all his criticisms of his own family down to just one thing it would be the complete lack of respect for personal space—physically *and* mentally. Every thought, every feeling, every pain, every movement was up for general discussion, dissection and in the worst-case scenario culminating in a family conference.

His middle sister, Celine, would even video call in from New Zealand, unwilling to let a small matter like time zones and distance prevent her from getting her two centimes' worth in.

The possibility of anybody in the Beaufils household not knowing the exact whereabouts of any member of their family at any given time was completely inconceivable. Sometimes Gabe suspected they had all been microchipped at birth. How could Polly Rafferty have no idea where her own twin brother was or what he was doing?

She looked up at him, the navy-blue eyes dark. 'I think I might be more jet-lagged than I realised,' she said slowly. 'Let me get this straight. You are working, here, at Rafferty's, as the vice CEO and living at Hopeford. In my house.'

'Temporarily,' Gabe clarified. 'Your house, that is.'

She closed her eyes.

A knock at the door jolted her back to wakefulness, the eyes snapping open.

'Yes?'

The door opened, followed a moment later by Rachel, who was carrying a large tray. She flickered a sympathetic glance over at Gabe and he couldn't resist winking back.

'Your coffee, Miss Rafferty.' Rachel set the tray onto the desk and smiled at Gabe. 'I brought your usual smoothie, Mr Beaufils,' she said in a much lighter tone. 'The chef has your muesli ready. I said you might prefer to eat it in the staff canteen this morning. Oh, and dry-cleaning has sent your clean shirt up. I'll just take it through for you.'

'*Merci*, Rachel.'

Polly had begun to pour her coffee but stopped

mid flow, her eyes narrowed and fixed on her assistant.

'You were aware that Mr Beaufils was here? In my office?'

'Well, he often works late...' Rachel said.

'And you didn't think to warn me?'

'I...'

'Tell Building Services I need to see them this morning. Mr Beaufils obviously needs his own sleeping and breakfasting area. Oh, and his own assistant. Get on to HR. We'll discuss the rest later.'

'Yes, Miss Rafferty.' Rachel bobbed out with a sigh of relief, returning a second later with a crisply wrapped shirt, which she handed to Gabe before exiting the office and closing the door.

'Nice girl, very competent.' Gabe sauntered over to the tray and picked up his usual smoothie. It had taken a few days for the chef to get the mixture just right but it was pretty close to perfection now. He took it over to the chaise and sipped but could feel Polly's eyes on him and looked over at her with a faintly enquiring smile.

'Are you quite comfortable?' she asked. 'Are you sure you don't want to ask for your muesli in here? Take a shower before getting dressed? How about a massage?'

He bit back a smile at the sarcastic tone in her voice. 'A shower would be lovely, thank you.' He downed the shake, feeling the cool liquid hit the back of his throat, the vitamins working their way into his system. 'Don't worry about showing me the way. I know my way around.'

'Hold on.' But she was too late, Gabriel Beaufils had disappeared into the cloakroom.

Polly jumped to her feet but came to a stop. She was hardly going to follow him into the shower, was she?

Not that he would mind—he'd probably just ask her to pass him the towel! After all he had no compunction about parading around her office half naked. No wonder Rachel was smitten. Smoothies and muesli indeed.

The phone on her desk blared. It was probably the kitchen wondering if Gabe wanted a lightly poached egg with his breakfast. Polly glared at it before pressing the speakerphone button.

'Polly Rafferty.'

'You're home, then.' Familiar grizzled, curt tones.

'Hello, Grandfather. I hope you're feeling better.' He at least hadn't expected her to go back to Hopeford before returning to work. But then Charles Rafferty had never actually taken a holiday—*his* bucket list probably read 'spend more time in the office'.

Her grandfather merely grunted. 'Hope you're ready to get down to some serious work after your little holiday.' Polly bit back the obvious retorts; it hadn't been a holiday, she had left the company after barely taking a long weekend off in the last five years.

But what was the point? Words wouldn't change him.

'Have you met Beaufils yet?'

Polly couldn't stop her eyes flicking towards the cloakroom door. 'I've seen him,' she said drily. 'Confident young man.'

'He's Vincent's boy, Gabriel. You know Chateau Deaufils of course, we've been their exclusive UK stockist for decades. He's the only son.'

'That doesn't explain why he's here.' Her voice was sharper than she had intended.

She didn't want her grandfather to know how much Gabe's presence had shaken her.

'Oh, he's not here because of the vineyard although that's a good connection of course. Man did some great things at Desmoulins, which is why I snapped him up. Thought he'd be good balance for you.'

'Good balance for me?' Polly wasn't sure whether she wanted to laugh or cry. Balance or replacement? If he couldn't have Raff did her grandfather want this young man instead? Just how much did she have to do before he finally accepted her? 'I really think I should have been consulted.'

'No.' Her grandfather's answer was as sharp as it was unequivocal. 'Vice CEO is a board decision. We need someone with different strengths from you, not someone you can ride roughshod over.'

Talk about the pot and the kettle. Polly glared at the phone.

'He knows the European markets and is very, very strong digitally, so I want him in charge of all e-commerce. Oh, and Polly? It's going to take a few weeks before his apartment is sound again. It won't bother you to have him at yours until then? You barely spend any time there as it is.'

Despite her best intentions Polly found her attention wandering back to the moment she had first seen Gabe sprawled on her chaise. The line of his back, the strong leanness of him, the delicacy of that intricate tattoo spiralling up his spine.

Thank goodness her grandfather wasn't here to see the flush on her cheeks.

Her first instinct was to demand they find Gabriel Beaufils alternative accommodation a long, long way from her house and home. And yet…it might be useful to keep him close. What was that they said about friends and enemies?

'I can't imagine there's much to excite him in Hopeford,' she said sweetly. 'But of course he can stay.'

The more she could find out about Gabriel Beaufils, the easier it would be to outmanoeuvre him. She was in charge of Rafferty's at last and no smoothie-drinking, bare-chested, charming Frenchman was going to change that.

CHAPTER TWO

GABE FINISHED TOWEL-DRYING his hair and grabbed the clean shirt Rachel had brought him. Pulling it on, he began to button it up slowly, once again running the morning's unexpected events through his mind. What had he been thinking?

He hadn't been thinking, that was the problem, he'd been reacting. A sure sign he'd allowed himself to mix business and pleasure that bit too often. Not enough sleep and too many office flirtations.

What a first impression! Although he wasn't sure what had thrown her more—the kiss or the news of his appointment.

He couldn't blame her for being less than pleased with either but he was here and he was staying put. Unlike Polly Rafferty he didn't have the advantage of bearing the founder's name, but he was just twenty-eight, already the vice CEO of Rafferty's and his goal of running his own company by thirty was looking eminently doable.

Things were nicely on track to get the results he needed, to learn everything he could and in two years look for the opportunity he needed to achieve his goal. Because life was short. Nobody knew that better than Gabe.

He pushed the thought away as he strode out of the bathroom and along the passage that led to the office. It was time to eat some humble pie.

'Nice shower?'

Gabe came to a halt and stared at Polly Rafferty. Was that a smile on her face?

'Rachel tells me you've been working all hours,' she continued. 'I just want to thank you. Obviously it was less than ideal that I wasn't back before Raff left but it's such a relief that you were here to help out.'

'I was more than happy to step in.' Gabe leant against the door frame and watched her through narrow eyes.

Polly seemed oblivious to his gaze. She was leaning back in his chair—correction, her chair—completely at her ease. She had taken off her jacket and it hung on the hat stand in the corner, her bag tossed carelessly on the floor beneath it. Her laptop was plugged into the keyboard and monitor, his own laptop folded and put aside. Several sheets of paper were stacked on the gleaming mahogany desk, a red pen lying on top of one, the crossed-out lines and scribbled notes implying great industry. It was as if she had never been away.

As if he had never been there.

Polly looked up, pen in hand. 'You haven't had breakfast so I suggest you take an hour or so while I get to grips with a few things here, then we can discuss how it's going to work moving forward. Starting with a permanent office and an assistant for you.' She couldn't be more gracious.

In fact she was the perfect hostess. Gabe suppressed a smile; he couldn't help approving of her tactics. Polly was throwing down the gauntlet. Oh, politely and with some degree of charm but, still, she was making it clear that absence or no absence this was her company and he was the incomer.

'You don't want your grandfather's office?' he asked. 'I assumed that you would want to move in there.'

A flicker of sadness ran over her face disturbing the blandly pleasant mask. 'This room belonged to my great-grandfather. The furniture and décor is just as it was, just as he chose. I'm staying here.'

But she wasn't going to offer him the bigger room either; he'd stake his reputation on it.

'I don't need an hour.' He pushed off the door frame. 'I am quite happy to start in fifteen minutes.'

'That's very sweet of you, Gabe.' The smile was back. 'But please, take an hour. I'll see you then.'

The dismissal was clear. Round one to Polly Rafferty.

That was okay. Gabe didn't care about individual rounds. He cared about the final prize. He inclined his head as he moved towards the door. 'Of course, take as long as you need to settle back in. Oh and, Polly? Welcome back.'

Polly held onto the smile as long as it took for the door to close behind the tall Frenchman then slumped forward with a sigh. It had taken her just a few minutes to reclaim the office but it still didn't feel like hers. It smelt different, of soap and a fresh citrusy cologne, of leather and whatever was in that disgusting green drink Gabe had tossed down so easily. She'd sniffed the glass when he was in the shower and recoiled in horror—until then she didn't think anything could be as vile as the look of the smoothie, but she'd been wrong.

Her coffee smelt off too. It must be the jet lag and all the travelling she'd done in the last week—nothing smelt right at the moment. Her stomach had twisted with nausea at the mere thought of caffeine or alcohol and even the eggs she had tried to eat at the airport.

Polly pushed the thought away. Whining that she was tired and that she felt ill wouldn't get her anywhere. She needed to hit the ground running and not stop.

Walking over to the massive art deco windows that dominated the office, she peered through their tinted panes at the street below. Coloured in red and green it looked like a film maker's whimsical view of the vibrant West End. Polly had always loved the strange slant the glass gave on the world. It helped her think clearly, think differently—helped her see problems in a new way.

And right now she needed all her wits about her.

'Gabriel Beaufils,' she said aloud, her mind conjuring up unbidden the tall man lounging at his ease, jeans riding low, bare chested, the water still dripping from his wet hair. What did that tell her?

That he was shameless. That he was beautiful.

Polly shook her head impatiently, replacing the image in her mind with the man that had just left. Leaning insouciantly against the door, wet hair slicked back. Still in jeans but now they were more sedately paired with a crisp white linen shirt. No tie. Laughter in his eyes.

That was better. Now what could she deduce from that? He didn't care what people thought about him, what she thought about him. That he was confident and utterly secure in his charm. That he was underestimating her.

She could work with that.

What else? Polly pulled herself away from the view and returned to her desk, running her fingers possessively over the polished wood. *Okay, let's do this.* She pulled up a search engine and typed in his name. 'Who are you, Monsieur Beaufils?' she murmured as she hit enter.

The page instantly filled with several engines. He had left quite the digital trail.

Polly sat back and began to read. Some of it she knew. He was from an affluent background, his family the proud makers of a venerable brand of wine. However, Gabe had left home in his late teens, gone to college in the States and stayed on to do his MBA while working at one of the biggest retail chains there.

'Good,' she muttered, returning to the results page and scanning the next paragraph, an article written about him just a few months ago. 'What else?'

Two years ago he had returned home to France, to Paris, to take charge of digital sales at Desmoulins. The young up-and-coming whizz-kid introducing innovation into one of Paris's most venerable *grande dames* had made quite a stir. Was that what he was planning to do here?

So much for his business history. Personal life? She moved through several lines of results. Nothing. Either he was very discreet or he didn't have a private life.

Polly's mouth tingled as if his lips were still hovering above hers. Despite herself she flicked her tongue over them as if she could still taste him. Discreet it was. That was a very practised kiss.

She took the cursor back to the top of the page and hit the images button. Instantly the page filled with photos of Gabe, smiling, serious, in a suit... in head-to-toe Lycra.

Hang on? He was wearing *what*?

She hovered over the image of Gabe walking out of a lake, wetsuit half undone, and Polly resisted the urge to zoom in on his chest. She checked the caption. He was a triathlete.

Gabriel Beaufils. Confident, charming, discreet and competitive.

She could handle that.

A smile curved her mouth. This was going to be almost too easy.

'I hope I didn't keep you waiting. I got caught up in something.'

As a matter of fact he was precisely on time— Polly would bet money that Gabe Beaufils had been standing outside the office watching a stopwatch to make sure he walked back in exactly one hour after she had dismissed him.

She would have done the same thing herself. Interesting.

Not that she was going to let him know that. She kept her eyes locked on her computer screen, giving every impression that she too was busy. 'I hope you had a nice breakfast.'

'Yes, thank you, most important meal of the day.' There was a dark hint of laughter in his voice.

'So they say.' She looked up and smiled. 'I'm usually too busy to remember to eat it.'

She had meant the glance and the smile to be brief, dismissive, but there was an intensity in his answering look that ensnared her. How could eyes be so dark, so knowing? Heat burned her cheeks, a shiver of awareness deep inside.

Reluctantly she pulled her gaze away, staring mindlessly at her computer screen, reading the same nonsensical sentence over and over again.

'You should take care of yourself, Polly.' His voice was low, caressing. 'Neglecting your body is not wise.'

'I don't neglect my body.' She wanted to pull the defensive words back as soon as she had uttered them.

'I exercise and eat well,' she clarified not entirely truthfully but she didn't want to admit to her snacking habits to him. Not when he was evidently so healthy. And fit. It took every ounce of willpower she had not to look up again, to sweep her eyes over him from head to toe, lingering on the muscles she knew were lurking under that crisp white shirt. 'I just don't make a big deal of it.'

She pushed her chair back and stood. 'I am going to do a walkabout,' she said. 'Would you care to accompany me?'

He stayed still for a moment, that curiously intent look still in his eyes, and then nodded courteously as he pulled the door open and held it for her.

Polly sensed his every movement as he followed her back out into the light, glass-walled foyer, awareness prickling her spine.

Rachel looked up as they walked by, curiosity clear on her face. Polly had no doubt that she was emailing all of her friends with a highly scurrilous account of her boss's encounter with a half-naked Frenchman. Let her; Polly would fill her PA's forthcoming days so completely that she wouldn't even be able to dream about gossiping.

It wasn't far from her office to one of the discreet doors that led out onto the shop floor. This was what Rafferty's was all about. No matter how essential the office functions were they existed for one purpose—to keep the iconic store in business. Polly ensured that every finance assistant, every marketing executive spent at least one week a year on the shop floor. Just as her great-grandfather had done. She herself spent most of December on the shop floor serving, restocking and assisting. The buzz and adrenaline rush were addictive.

'I've spoken to Building Services,' she said as she slid her pass through the door lock, turning with one hand on the handle to face Gabe. 'I am going to turn Grandfather's old office into the boardroom. It's bigger than any of the meeting rooms, far too big for one person—and I think he'll be pleased with the gesture. He is still President of the Board.'

Polly knew everyone expected her to move into the vast corner suite but couldn't face the thought of occupying her grandfather's chair, feeling him second-guessing her all the time, disapproving of every change she made.

'And me?' It was said with a self-deprecating and very Gallic shrug but Polly wasn't fooled. There was a sharpness in his eyes.

'The old boardroom.' It was a neat solution.

Polly got to keep her office, her grandfather would hopefully feel honoured and Gabe would get a brand-new office in keeping with his position. But not a Rafferty office, not one with history steeped in its walls.

'Building Services are confident they can create a room for your assistant with no major infrastructure changes and there's already a perfectly good cloakroom. You can start picking wallpaper and furniture this week and it should be ready end of next week.'

'And where do I work in the meantime?' His voice was still mild but Polly was aware of a stillness about him, a quiet confidence in his gaze. She didn't want to push too far, not yet. Reluctantly she discarded her plan that he sit in her foyer, with Rachel, or that she find him a spare desk in one of the bigger, open-plan offices where the rest of the backroom staff worked.

'We can fit a second desk in my room,' she said. 'Just until you're settled. But, Gabe? No more sleeping in the office, no more using my assistant to sort out your laundry and...' she swallowed but kept her gaze and voice firm '...you remain fully dressed and act appropriately at all times. Understood?'

Gabe's mouth quirked. 'Of course,' he murmured.

'Good.' She pushed the door open.

This was it, this was where the magic happened.

Polly blinked as she stepped out. They had entered the home furnishings department on the top floor and the lights were switched to full, purposely dazzling to best showcase the silks, cushions, throws, ceramics, silverware and all the other luxury items Rafferty's told their customers were essential for a comfortable home. Beneath them were floors and galleries devoted to technology, books, toys, food and, of course, fashion.

Polly's heart swelled and she clenched her fists. She was home.

And yet everything had changed. She had changed.

She had hoped that being back would ground her again but it was odd walking through the galleries with Gabe. If her staff greeted her with their usual respect, they greeted him with something warmer.

And how on earth did he know every name after what? Three or four weeks?

'*Bonjour*, Emily.' Polly narrowed her eyes at him as they entered the world-famous haberdashery room. Had his accent thickened as he greeted the attractive redhead who had turned the department into the must-go destination for a new generation of craft lovers?

'How is your cat? Did the operation go well?' He had moved nearer to Emily, smiling down at her intimately.

Polly's head snapped round. No way. He knew the names of every staff member and all about the health of their pets too?

'Yes, thank you, Mr Beaufils, she's desperate to go outside but she's doing really well.' Emily was smiling back, her voice a little breathy.

'They can be such a responsibility, *non*? I 'ave...'

Had he just dropped an aitch? *Really?* Polly had known him for what, an hour? And she already knew perfectly well that Gabe spoke perfect, almost accentless English. Unless, it seemed, he was talking to petite redheads. She coughed and could have sworn she saw a glimmer of laughter in the depths of his almost-black eyes as he continued.

'I 'ave been looking after Mademoiselle Rafferty's cat for the last few weeks. He is a rascal, that one. Such a huge responsibility.'

'They are,' Emily said earnestly, her huge eyes fixed on his. 'But worth it.'

'*Oui*, the way they purr. So trusting.'

That was it. Polly felt ill just listening. 'So greedy,' she said briskly. 'And so prone to eviscerating small mammals under the bed. If you're ready, Gabe, shall we continue? Nice work,' she said to Emily, unable to keep a sarcastic tone from her voice. 'Keep it up.' And without a backwards glance she swept from the department.

It had been an interesting morning. Gabe was well aware that he had been well and truly sized up, tested and judged. What the verdict was he had no idea.

Nor, truth be told, was he that interested. He had his own weighing up to do.

Tough, but not as tough as she thought. Surprisingly stylish for someone who lived and breathed work; the sharp little suit she was wearing would pass muster in the most exclusive streets in Paris—unusual for an Englishwoman. He liked how she wasn't afraid of her height, accentuating it with heels, the blonde hair swept up into a knot adding an extra couple of centimetres.

And she wasn't going to give him an inch. The solution to the offices was masterful. It was going to be fun working with her.

He loved a good game.

Gabe strode through the foyer, smiling at Rachel as she looked up with a blush. Maybe he should have gone a little easier on the flirting. He wouldn't make that mistake with his own assistant—he would request a guy or, even better, a motherly woman who would keep all unwanted callers away and feed him home-made cake. He made a note to keep an eye on the 'interests' section of any applicants' CVs.

He opened the door to Polly's office without knocking; after all they were sharing it.

'This is going to be fun,' he said as Polly looked up from her computer screen, trying unsuccessfully to hide her irritation at the interruption. 'Roomies, housemates. We should take a road trip too, complete the set.'

Bed mates would really make it a full hand but he wasn't going to suggest that. Totally inappropriate. But, despite himself, his eyes wandered over her face, skimming over the smattering of freckles high on her cheeks, the wide mouth, the pointed little chin. She kissed like she spoke— with passion and purpose—but there was none of the coolness and poise. No, there was heat simmering away behind that cool façade.

Heat he was better off pretending he knew nothing about.

'I'll let you have a lift in the company car. Will that do?' She looked unamused. 'Did you decide on office furniture? There's a temporary desk for you there.' She nodded over towards the wall where a second desk had already been set up, a monitor and phone installed on its gleaming surface.

'I'll be here a week or two at the most according to Building Services and then you're free of me.'

'Hardly,' she muttered so low he could barely make out her words then spoke out in her usual crisp tones. 'Are you available to talk now?'

'*Certainement*, if you need me to be.' He didn't mean to let his voice drop or to drawl the words out quite so suggestively but the colour rising swiftly in her cheeks showed their effect all too clearly. 'It would be good to start again, properly,' he clarified.

'Good.' Polly waited until he had taken his seat at his new desk. It wasn't quite as good a position as hers, which faced the incredible windows. When Gabe had sat there absorbed in his work he would look absently up every so often, only to be struck anew by the light, the simple artistry of the stylised floral design.

Now his view was the bookshelves that lined the opposite wall—and Polly, her desk directly in his eyeline. She swivelled her chair towards him, a notepad and pen poised in her hand, her legs crossed.

The only way this was going to work was if he behaved himself in thought and deed. But he was a mere man after all and better souls than him would find it hard to stop their gaze skimming over the long willowy figure and the neatly crossed legs. Incredibly long, ridiculously shapely legs. Of course they were.

'You've got a pretty impressive CV,' she said finally. 'Why Rafferty's?'

'That means a lot coming from you,' he said honestly. 'Oh, come on,' as her brows rose in surprise. 'Polly Rafferty, you set the standard, you must know that. I came here to work with you.'

'With me?'

'Don't misunderstand me, there's a lot you can learn from me as well. In some ways Rafferty's is stuck in the Dark Ages, especially digitally. But, you have done some great things here over the last few years. I have no problem admitting there are still things I need to learn if I am going to be a CEO by the time I'm thirty...'

'Here?'

He raised an eyebrow. 'Would you let me?'

'You'd have to kill me first.' She shook her head, her colour high.

'That's what I thought. No, maybe a start-up, or even my own business. I'll see nearer the time.'

'You're ambitious. It took me until I was thirty-one to make it.' Her eyes met his coolly, the blue of her eyes dark.

'I know.' He grinned. 'A little competition keeps me focused.' He shrugged. 'Rafferty's is possibly the most famous store in Europe if not the world. It's the missing piece in my experience—and I have a lot to offer you as well. It's a win-win situation.'

She leant back. 'Prove it. What would you change?'

He grinned. 'Are you ready for it? You only just got back.'

The corners of her mouth turned up, the smallest of smiles. 'Don't pull your punches. I can take it.'

'Okay then.' He jumped out of the chair and began to pace up and down the room. It was always easier to think on his feet; those months of being confined to bed had left him with a horror of inaction.

'Your social media lacks identity and your online advertising is practically non-existent—it's untargeted and unplanned, effectively just a redesign of your print advertising. I suggest you employ a digital marketing consultant to train your existing staff. Emily is very capable. She just needs guidance and some confidence.'

He looked across for a reaction but she was busy scribbling notes. Gabe rolled his eyes. 'This is part of the problem. You're what? Writing longhand?'

'I think better with paper and pen. I'll type them up later.' Her voice was defensive.

'*Non*, the whole company needs to think digitally. The sales force need tablets so they can check sizes and styles at the touch of a button, mix and match styles.'

'We have a personal touch here. We don't need to rely on tablets…'

'You need both,' he said flatly. 'But what you really need is a new website.'

There was a long moment of incredulous silence. 'But it's only three years old. Do you *know* how much we spent on it?'

Polly was no longer leaning back. She was ramrod-straight, her eyes sparkling, more in anger than excitement, Gabe thought. 'Too much and it's obsolete. Come on, Polly.' His words tumbled over each other, his accent thickened in his effort to convince her.

'Do you want a website that's fine and gets the job done or do you want one that's a window into the very soul of Rafferty's? You have no other stores anywhere—this is it. Your Internet business *is* your worldwide business and that's where the expansion lies.'

'What do you have in mind?'

This was what made him tick, made his blood

pump, the adrenaline flow—planning, innovating, creating. It was better than finishing a marathon, hell, sometimes it was better than sex. 'A site that is visually stunning, one that creates the feel and the look of the store as much as possible. Each department would be organised by gallery, exactly as you are laid out here so that customers get to experience the look, the feel of Rafferty's—but virtually. Online assistants would be available twenty-four hours to chat and advise and, most importantly, the chance to personalise the experience. Why should people buy from Rafferty's online when there are hundreds, thousands of alternatives?'

She didn't answer, probably couldn't.

'If we make it better than all the rest then Rafferty's is the store that customers will choose. They can upload their measurements, their photos and have virtual fittings—that way, they can order with certainty, knowing that the clothes will fit and suit them. Cut down on returns and make the whole shopping experience fun and interactive.'

'How much?'

'It won't be cheap,' he admitted. 'Not to build, maintain or staff. But it will be spectacular.'

She didn't speak for a minute or so, staring straight ahead at the window before nodding decisively. 'There's a board meeting next week. Can you have a researched and costed paper ready for then?'

Researched *and* costed? *'Oui.'* If he had to work all day and night. 'So, what about you?'

'What about me?'

'There must be something you want to do, something to stamp your identity firmly on the store.'

'I have been running the company for the last year,' she reminded him, her voice a little frosty.

'But now it's official…' If she wasn't itching to make some changes he had severely underestimated her.

She didn't answer for a moment, her eyes fixed unseeingly on the windows. 'We have never expanded,' she said after a while. 'We always wanted to keep Rafferty's as a destination store, somewhere people could aspire to visit. And it works, we're on so many tourist tick lists; they buy teddies or tea in branded jars, eat in the tea room and take their Rafferty's bag home. And with the Internet there isn't any real need for bricks-and-mortar shops elsewhere.'

'But?'

'But we've become a little staid,' Polly said. She rolled her shoulders as she spoke, stretching out her neck. Gabe tried not to stare, not to notice how graceful her movements were, as she turned her attention to her hair, unpinning it and letting the dark blonde tendrils fall free.

Polly sighed, running her fingers through her hair before beginning to twist it back into a looser, lower knot. It felt almost voyeuristic standing there watching her fingers busy themselves in the tangle of tresses.

'We were one of the first stores in London to stock bikinis. Can you imagine—amidst the post-war austerity, the rationing and a London still two decades and a generation from swinging... my great-grandfather brought several bikinis over from Paris. There were letters of outrage to *The Times*.

'We were the first to unveil the latest trends, to sell miniskirts. We were *always* cutting edge and now we're part of a tour that includes Buckingham Palace and Madame Tussauds.' The contempt was clear in her voice. 'We're doing well financially, really well, but we're no longer cutting edge. We're safe, steady, middle-aged.' Polly wrinkled her nose as she spoke.

It was true; Rafferty's was a byword for elegance, taste and design but not for innovation, not any more. Even Gabe's own digital vision could only sell the existing ranges. But it was fabulously profitable with a brand recognition that was through the roof; wasn't that enough? 'Can a store this size actually be cutting edge any more? Surely that's the Internet's role...'

'I disagree.' She shook her head vehemently. 'We have the space, the knowledge, the passion and the history. The problem is, it takes a lot for us to take on a new designer or a new range, to hand over valuable floor space to somebody little known and unproven—and if they have already established themselves then we're just following, not innovating.'

'So, what do you plan to do about it?' This was more like it. Her eyes were focused again, sharp.

'Pop-ups.'

'Pardon?'

'Pop-ups. Bright, fun and relatively low cost. We can create a pop-up area in store for new designers whether it's clothes, jewellery, shoes—

we'll champion new talent right here at Rafferty's. Sponsor a graduate show during London fashion week in the main gallery.'

That made a lot of sense.

'But I don't just want to draw people here. I want to go out and find them—it could be a great opportunity to take Rafferty's out of the city as well. Where do we have the biggest footfall?'

It was a good thing he'd pulled those eighteen-hour days; he could answer with utter confidence. 'The food hall.'

'Exactly! The British are finally understanding food—no, don't pull a superior gourmet French face at me. They are and you know it. There are hundreds of food festivals throughout the country and I want us to start having a presence at the very best of them. And not just food festivals. I want us at Glyndebourne, Henley, the Edinburgh Festival Fringe. Anywhere there's a buzz I want Rafferty's. Exclusive invitation-only previews to create excitement, with takeaway afternoon teas and Rafferty's hampers—filled with a selection of our bestselling products as souvenirs.'

Gabe rubbed his chin. 'Will it make a profit?'

'Yes, but not a massive one,' she conceded. 'But

it *will* revitalise us, introduce us to the younger market who may think we're too staid for them. Make us more current and more exciting. And that market will be your domestic digital users.'

Gabe could feel it, the roar of adrenaline, the tightening in his gut that meant something new, something exhilarating was in the air. 'It would create a great buzz on social media.'

She nodded, her whole face lit up. 'It all works together, doesn't it? I am presenting at the board meeting too. It's less investment up front than you will need—but this is something untried and untested and the current board are a little conservative. You support me and, once I've checked your finances and conclusions, I'll support your digital paper. We'll have a lot more impact if we're united. Deal?' She held out her hand.

Gabe worked alone. He preferred it that way. Sure, he had good relationships with his colleagues, liked to make sure they were all onside but he didn't want or brook interference.

Freedom at home and at work. That way he never had to worry about letting anyone down.

But this was a great opportunity—to be part of the team dragging Rafferty's into a new age.

How could he refuse? He took her hand, cool and elegant just like its owner.

'Deal.'

CHAPTER THREE

POLLY KICKED OFF her shoes with a sigh of relief. She was home, the sun was shining and it was Friday evening. This was exactly what she needed to get over this pesky jet lag. Surely the tiredness, the constant nausea and the lack of appetite should have gone by now?

It wasn't exactly a weekend break, she still had a lot of work to do if she was to wow the board in a week's time, but she could do it at home either in the little sunshine-drenched study at the back of the cottage or in the timber-beamed, book-lined sitting room. Away from the office.

Usually her office was a sanctuary but right now it felt alien. Gabe seemed to fill every corner of it. His gym gear in her cloakroom, a variety of equally disgusting smoothies on the table and, worst of all, Gabe himself.

He was so *active*, always on the phone, pacing

round, chatting to every member of staff as if they were his long-lost best friend.

Even his typing was a loud, banging, flamboyant display. She couldn't think, couldn't concentrate when he was in the room.

But, although he had been living in Hopeford, in her house, for several weeks there was no trace of Gabe in the living areas of the cottage; his few possessions were kept neatly put away in the guest bedroom. Not that she'd snooped, obviously, but she had felt a need to reacquaint herself with her home, visiting every room, reminding herself of its quirks and corners.

It was odd being back after such a long absence. The cottage was clean, aired and well stocked, the rambling garden weeded and watered all thanks to the concierge service she employed to take care of her home. Mr Simpkins, the handsome ginger cat she'd inherited when she'd bought the house, was plump and sleek and bearing no discernible grudge after their time apart. But everything felt smaller, more claustrophobic.

For three months she had been someone else. Someone with no purpose, no expectations. It had been disconcerting and yet so freeing.

But that was over. She was home now and she had a lot to do. Friday night usually meant her laptop, a glass of wine and a takeaway. Polly put her hand to her stomach and swallowed hard; maybe she'd forego the latter two this week.

And think about a doctor's appointment if the tiredness and nausea didn't go away soon.

Hang on a second, what was that? Polly had visitors so rarely that it took another sharp decisive peal of the doorbell before she moved. Probably Gabe.

'If he can't keep hold of his keys how can I trust him with Rafferty's online strategy?' she asked Mr Simpkins. He merely yawned and turned over, stretching out in a patch of early evening sunshine.

Walking down the wide stairs towards the hallway, she took a moment to look around; at the polished, oiled beams, the old flagstoned floor, the gilt mirror by the hat stand, the fresh flowers on the antique table. It had all been chosen, placed and cared for by someone else. She lived here but was it really hers?

The doorbell rang again, impatiently. 'I'm coming,' she called, trying to keep the irritation out of her voice. It was hardly her fault that he had forgotten his keys. Unlocking the door, she pulled it open.

It wasn't Gabe.

Tall, broad, hair the same colour as hers and eyes the exact same shade of dark blue. A face she knew as well as she knew her own. A face she hadn't seen in four years. Polly clung onto the door frame, disbelief flooding through her. 'Raff?'

'I still have a key.' He held it up. 'But I didn't think you'd want me just walking in.'

'But, what are you doing here? I thought you were in Jordan. Or Australia?'

'Sorry to disappoint you. Can I come in?'

'Sorry?' Polly gaped at him as his words sank in. 'Yes, of course.'

She stepped back, her mind still grasping for a reason her twin brother was here in her sleepy home town, not trying to save the world, one war zone at a time.

Raff faced her, the love and warmth in his eyes bringing a lump to her throat. How on earth had four years gone by since she had last seen him? 'Come here.' He took her in his arms. It had been so long since he had held her, since she had allowed herself to lean on him.

'It's so good to see you,' he said into her hair. Polly tightened her grip.

It wasn't Raff's fault their grandfather had favoured him, wanted him to take over the store. Yet somehow it had been easier to hold him culpable.

'Hi, heavenly twin,' she murmured and took comfort in his low rumble of laughter. They had been named for the Heavenly Twins, Castor and Pollux, but Polly had escaped with a feminine version of her name. Her brother had been less lucky; nobody, apart from their grandparents, used it— Raff preferred a shorter version of their surname.

'Thanks for looking after everything.' She disentangled herself slowly, although the temptation to lean in and not let go was overwhelming. She led him down the wide hallway towards the kitchen. 'Looking after the house, Mr Simpkins.' She swallowed, hard and painful. 'Taking over at Rafferty's.'

'You needed my help, of course I stepped in.' He paused. 'I wish you'd called, Pol. Told me what was going on. I didn't mind but it would have been good if we had worked together, sorted it out together.'

'After four years? I couldn't,' she admitted, heading over to the fridge so that she didn't have to face him. 'You stayed away, Raff. You went away, left me behind and you didn't come back. Ever.' She swallowed painfully. 'I didn't even know whose side you were on—if you had spoken to Grandfather, knew what he was planning, if you wanted Rafferty's.' That had been her worst fear, that her twin had colluded with her grandfather.

Raff sounded incredulous. 'Surely you didn't think I would agree? That I would take Rafferty's away from you?'

'Grandfather made it very clear that nothing I had done, nothing I could do was enough to compete with your Y chromosome.' She turned, forced herself to meet the understanding in his eyes. 'It destroyed me.'

Raff winced. 'Polly, I spent three months running Rafferty's while you were gone and I hated every minute of it. How you manage I don't know. But even if I had come back and experienced an epiphany about the joys of retail I *still* wouldn't have agreed. I don't deserve it and you do. You've worked for it, you live it, love it. Even Grandfather had to admit in the end that his desire to see me in Father's place was wrong, that his fierce determination for a male heir was utterly crazy. I've agreed to join the board as a family member but that's it. You're CEO, you're in charge.'

Polly grabbed a cold beer and threw it to her twin, who caught it deftly with one hand, and pulled out a bottle of white wine for herself. She checked the label: Chateau Beaufils Chardonnay Semillon. One of Gabe's, then.

'So where have you been?' Raff was leaning against the kitchen counter. He raised the beer. 'Cheers.'

'Oh, here and there.' Polly's cheeks heated up and she busied herself with looking for a corkscrew. *Remember the new bucket list,* she told herself, ruthlessly pushing the more reprehensible details of her time away out of her mind. 'I went backpacking. In South America.' She flashed him a smile. 'Just like you always said I should.'

He smirked. 'When you say backpacking, you mean five-star hotels and air-conditioned tours?'

'Sometimes,' Polly admitted, breathing a sigh

of relief as the stubborn cork finally began to give way. She eased it out carefully, wrinkling her nose as the aroma hit her. She held the bottle out to Raff. 'Is this corked?'

He took it and inhaled. 'I don't think so.'

She shrugged, and poured a small amount into a glass. She didn't sip it though; just the sight of the straw-coloured liquid caused her stomach to roll ominously. She put the glass down. 'But I did my fair share of rucksacks and walking boots too, along the Inca trail and other places.' She grinned across at him. 'You wouldn't have recognised me, braids in my hair, a sarong, all my worldly goods in one bag.'

'I had no idea where you were.' He didn't sound accusatory; he didn't need to. She had read his emails, listened to his voicemails. She knew how much worry she'd caused him.

'I didn't want you to. I didn't want pity or advice or anything but time to figure out who I was, who I wanted to be if I wasn't going to run Rafferty's.'

'And?'

'I was still figuring it out when Clara emailed me telling me to come home. So, don't think I'm not glad to see you but why are you here? Did you miss Mr Simpkins?'

'My shirts don't look the same without a covering of ginger fur,' he agreed. 'Polly, there's something I need to tell you.' He turned his beer bottle round and round, his gaze fixed on it. 'I'm not going to be working in the field any more. I've accepted a job at the headquarters of Doctors Everywhere instead and I'm moving here, to Hopeford.'

Polly stared. 'But you love your job. Why on earth would you change it? And you're moving here? Hang on!' She looked at him suspiciously. 'Do you want to move back in? I'm not running a doss centre for young executive males who are quite capable of finding their own places, you know.'

'For who?' His face cleared. 'Oh, Gabe? He's still here? How are you getting on with him?'

'No.' She shook her head, unwilling to discuss her absent houseguest. 'No changing the subject. What's going on?'

Raff took a deep breath. 'You're not the only one who's been working things out recently. I have to admit I was pissed when you left with no word— I hotfooted it straight here, convinced that Clara knew where you were. I was determined to get it out of her, drag you back and get on with my life.'

'She didn't. I didn't even really know what my plans were.'

His mouth twisted into a smile. 'I know that now but things were a bit hostile for a while.' He shook his head. 'I can't believe it's only been a few months since I met her, that there was a time I didn't know her. Thing is, Pol, meeting Clara changed everything. I'm engaged. That's why I'm staying in the UK, that's why I'm moving to Hopeford. I'm marrying Clara.'

'Bonsoir?'

Polly should get off the sofa, should open her laptop, look as if she were working.

But she couldn't. Her appetite for the game, the competition had gone.

'Hi.' She looked up wearily as Gabe walked into the room. He was so tall his head nearly brushed the beams on the low ceiling.

'Nice run?' she continued. Small talk was good; it was easy. It stopped her having to think.

'Oui.' He stretched, seemingly unaware that his T-shirt was riding up and exposing an inch of flat,

toned abdomen. 'A quick ten kilometres. It ruins the buzz though, getting the train after. I might try biking back to Hopeford one evening. What is it? Just fifty kilometres?'

'Just,' she echoed.

Gabe looked at her curiously. 'Are you okay?'

'Yes, no.' She gave a wry laugh. 'I don't really know. Raff's engaged.'

'Your brother? That's amazing. We should celebrate.'

'We should,' she agreed.

The dark eyes turned to her, their expression keen. 'You're not happy?'

'Of course I am,' Polly defended herself and then sighed. 'I am,' she repeated. 'It's just he's moving here, to Hopeford. He's marrying my closest friend and joining the board at Rafferty's.'

She shook her head. 'I feel like I am being a total cow,' she admitted. 'It's just, I have spent my whole life competing against him—and he wins without even taking part.

'And now...' she looked down at her hands '...now he's moving to my town, will be on the board of my company and is marrying the one person I can confide in. It feels like there's nowhere I am just me, not Raff's twin sister.'

The silence stretched out between them.

'I have three sisters,' he said after a while. 'I'm the youngest. It can be hard to find your place.'

Polly looked over at him. 'Is that why you're here? Not working at the vineyard?'

'Partly. And because I needed to prove some things to myself.' He walked over to Mr Simpkins, who was lying on the cushion-covered window seat set into the wall on the far side of the chimney breast.

Gabe should have been an incongruous presence in the white-walled, book-lined sitting room, the soft furnishings and details were so feminine, so English country cottage. He was too young, too indisputably French, too tall, too *male* for the low-beamed, cosy room. And yet he looked utterly at home reaching over to run one hand down Mr Simpkins' spine.

He was wearing jeans, his dark hair falling over his forehead, his pallor emphasised by the deep shadows under his dark eyes and the black stubble covering his jaw. He worked so late each night, rising at dawn to fit in yet another session in the gym—and the lack of sleep showed.

Polly watched the long, lean fingers' firm caress as her cat flattened himself in suppliant pleasure and felt a jolt in the pit of her stomach, a sudden insistent ache of desire as her nerve endings re-membered the way his hand had settled in the curve of her waist, those same fingers moving up along her body, making her purr almost as loudly as Mr Simpkins.

'Is that why you went away?' he asked, all his attention seemingly on the writhing cat. 'Because of your brother?'

Polly flushed, partly in shame at having to admit her own second-class status to a relative stranger—and half in embarrassment at her re-action to the slow, sure strokes from Gabe's capable-looking hands.

'Partly,' she admitted. 'I had to get away, learn who I was without Rafferty's.'

'And did you?' He looked directly at her then, his eyes almost black and impossibly dark. 'Learn who you are?'

Polly thought back. To blisters and high alti-tudes. To the simple joy of a shower after a five-day trek. To long twilight walks on the beach. To lying back and watching the stars, the balmy breeze warm on her bare skin. To the lack of responsibility. To taking risks.

It had been fun but ultimately meaningless.

'No,' she said. 'I saw some amazing things, did amazing things and I had fun. But there was nothing to find out. Without Rafferty's I don't have anything…I'm no one.'

'That's not true.' His voice was low, intimate.

'It is,' she argued. 'But Raff? He is utterly and completely himself. I think I've always envied that. And now he has Clara—which is great, she's lovely and I'm sure they'll be very happy. But my brother and best friend getting married? It leaves me with no one.'

She heard her words echo as she said them and flushed. 'I am the most selfish beast, ignore me, Gabe. I'm tired and fluey and having a pathetic moment. It'll pass!'

He regarded her quietly. 'And you don't eat,' he said after a while. 'Come on, I'll cook.'

Polly was still protesting as Gabe rummaged through the fridge, trying to find something he could make into a meal a Frenchman could be proud of. It might have to be a simple omelette, he decided, pulling the eggs out of the fridge along with a courgette, some cheese and the end of some chorizo.

'You really don't have to cook for me,' she said. 'I'm quite happy with some bread and cheese.'

'Do you ever cook?' He looked at the gleaming range cooker, the beautiful copper saucepans hanging from their hooks looking as blemish free as the day they were bought.

'I butter bread and slice cheese. Occasionally I shred a lettuce.'

'That is some variety.'

'I know.'

He continued to chop onions as she watched.

'So you're a business whizz-kid, a gourmet chef, a triathlete. Is there anything you can't do?'

'I've never backpacked.'

'Didn't fancy the dirt and blisters?'

'I didn't have the time.' Gabe scraped the onions into the pan and tipped it expertly so they were evenly covered in oil. 'I went to university late and had a lot of time to make up. No chance to slack off.'

Polly was sitting at the counter, her chin propped in her hands. 'Is that why you set yourself such a punishing schedule now?'

Was it? All Gabe knew was that once you'd spent a year confined to bed, without the strength to get a glass of water, watching your classmates grow up without you, that once you knew just what losing someone meant then you had to make the most of every single second.

'You can sleep when you're dead,' he said. It was all too true; he'd thought about that long enough.

Now he just wanted to live every moment.

Polly continued to watch as he whisked the eggs. 'What do your parents think? Of you working away? Did they expect you to work with them?'

Ouch, that was direct. 'They found it hard to adjust.' He poured the eggs into the pan with a flourish. 'They wanted me to go to university nearby, stay in Provence. When I said I was going to Boston they were hurt. But they got over it.'

On the surface at least. The very worst part of being ill had been the despair in his parents' faces whenever they thought he wasn't watching. Or the forced positivity when they knew he was. It made it hard to say no to them.

'You're the son and heir.' There was no hiding the bitterness in her words. 'Of course they expect a lot.'

His mouth curved into a wry smile. 'Son? *Oui.* Heir? That remains to be seen. Celine is studying vineyard management in New Zealand and Claire is doing a very good job of opening the chateau up to guests and tourists while presenting them with a perfect trio of grandchildren.'

'Three!' She straightened up, pulling her hair back into a knot as she did so. He watched, fascinated, as she gathered up the silky golden strands and twisted them ruthlessly, tucking the end under. It wouldn't take much to make it spill free. Just one touch.

'Three in three years,' he confirmed. 'And Natalie is expecting her second. She takes care of all the advertising and marketing. So you see I have some formidable rivals for the vineyard. If I wanted it that is.'

'Isn't it funny? You and Raff could have it all on a plate. And you don't even want it.'

'We still have to work,' he argued. 'No one I work with cares what my parents do. Raff had to work his way up at Doctors Everywhere. It's exactly the same. Pass me a plate, will you?'

Polly got up and took two plates off the dresser, handing them over. Gabe shredded some lettuce and added a couple of tomatoes before cutting the omelette in half and sliding it onto a plate.

'*Voilà,*' he said, sliding it towards her.

'Thanks, Gabe, this looks great.' Her hair was coming loose and she gathered it up again, beginning the familiar twisting motion as she re-knotted it, before picking up her fork.

'I have worked at Rafferty's since I was legally allowed to get a job. Before that I spent every moment there.' Her voice was wistful, filled with love.

Gabe pictured the iconic store, its large dome and art deco façade dominating the expensive London street on which it was situated. It was always busy, exuding wealth and glamour and style. Exciting and as restless as its patrons, prowling in search of the bag, the outfit, the décor that would make them unique, special. It was easy to see why she loved it.

But then his mind turned to the chateau, to the acres and acres of vines, the scent of lavender and the scarlet flash of poppies. The old grey building, covered in ivy. He loved the buzz of retail but had to admit that no shop, no matter how magical, could match his home. The look in her eyes, the note in her voice spoke of the same deep connection.

'It's your home,' he said.

'Yes!' Polly pointed her fork at him. 'That's it. But only temporarily. It was made very clear to me that I could work there but it was never going to be mine. Grandfather even wanted me to study History of Art instead of business, not that I took any notice of him.'

So much dwelling on the past; if Gabe had done that he would still be in Provence, weeping in the graveyard. 'But now look at you. In charge of the whole store.'

Polly took a bite of the omelette, her face thoughtful. 'I told you I went away to find myself. The truth is I had no choice. Grandfather came to see me three months ago and told me he was signing Rafferty's over to Raff.' She laughed but there was no humour in the sound.

'My ex had just got engaged and Grandfather was concerned for me, or so he said. He thought

I was leaving it too late, "letting the good ones get away".' She swallowed. 'He said it was for my own good—I should concentrate on marriage, have children before it's too late.'

'That was unkind.'

'It hurt me.' It obviously still did, her voice and her face full of pain. 'So I left my job, my home and I went away to try and work out who I was without Rafferty's. But then Raff walked away, for good this time, and I came back.'

She looked at Gabe, a gleam of speculation in her eyes. 'I have to admit I was thrown when I got back to find you already in place. At first I thought Grandfather was trying to replace Raff, but now?' She shook her head, once more dislodging the precarious knot of hair, 'I wonder what kind of game he's playing.'

'Maybe, he just knows I'm good at my job.'

'Oh, that will be part of it,' she agreed. 'But with Raff engaged I'll bet there's something else. It wouldn't be the first time he's played matchmaker. You've got to admit it's convenient, working together, living together.' Her voice trailed off.

'And I thought it was an over-ambitious devel-

oper tunnelling under my building. Your grandfather must have some extraordinary powers.'

'You have no idea,' Polly said darkly. 'He's
pretty unscrupulous.' She shook her head. 'He
just can't stop interfering.'

'You are just speculating. Besides, what does
it matter? He can play all he wants.' Gabe made
an effort to speak calmly but his heart was thudding so loudly he was surprised the kitchen wasn't
shaking. Marriage? Children? If Charles Rafferty
was looking at Gabe to fulfil his dynastic dreams
he had a long, long wait ahead. 'We don't have to
join in. Not on his terms.'

Light, fun and short-lived. That was all he
wanted, all he could cope with. Polly Rafferty
was many impressive things but were light and
fun part of her enticing package? She hid it well
if so.

But getting under her skin *was* fun. He was
pretty sure, by the way her gaze lingered on his
mouth, by the sudden flush that highlighted her
cheeks occasionally, that she hadn't forgotten
about that kiss.

And he certainly hadn't—not for want of trying.

'Of course we don't.' She sounded more like her

usual self. 'I've never allowed myself to follow the path Grandfather thinks suitable. I'm not going to start now he has finally retired. I'm still so tired, I'm probably imagining things. You're not my type at all. Even Grandfather must see that.'

This was where a wise man would stay silent. 'I'm not?'

The soft words caught her, echoing round and around her head.

'Of course not, you're an exercise-mad smoothie drinker who flirts inappropriately with half my staff.' Polly tried to keep her voice light but she could feel inappropriate heat rushing to her cheeks, a sweet insistent ache pulsing in her chest, reverberating all the way down to the pit of her stomach. She didn't want to look at him yet somehow she had turned, caught in his dark gaze, 'Not to mention that we work together.'

Had he leaned in closer? The dark eyes were even more intent than usual, black pools she was drawn to, the kind of bottomless depths girls could drown in. 'I won't tell if you don't.'

'Tell what?' But her tone lacked conviction even to herself. 'Gabe, I…' Polly wasn't entirely sure what she had been planning to say, whether she was going to lean in, close the distance between them and pull him in close—or turn away and tell him to grow up and stop with the innuendoes. She knew the sensible choice, the logical choice and yet she hesitated.

But the kitchen seemed to have shrunk, the space suddenly, suffocatingly small, the air so stuffy she could hardly breathe, the tumult in her stomach churning. She gasped for a breath, realising her mistake too late, pushing her stool back and running for the downstairs cloakroom horrifyingly aware that she wasn't going to make it.

'I am so humiliated.' Polly leant forward until her forehead touched the kitchen counter, grateful for the coolness of the granite. 'Thank you for taking care of me.'

That wasn't quite enough but she didn't want to articulate all the reasons for her gratitude. The gentle way he had rubbed her back, held her hair back from her face, waited with her until the last spasm had passed. 'You're good with sick people.' She looked up and smiled but he didn't return her admittedly pathetic attempt, his eyes filled with an unexpected pain.

'I have some experience.' His face was unreadable but his voice was gentle.

'I wasn't drunk.' Bad enough that it had happened; it would be far worse if he thought she was some kind of lush.

'You hadn't eaten. Even one glass could have that effect.' He looked at the glass she had poured earlier.

'I didn't even have one sip,' she protested. 'Just the smell made me feel ill. I must have picked up some kind of bug.'

He put a hand on her shoulder, just that one light touch sending shivers down her spine. 'You should eat something now, some crackers maybe.'

'No.' Not crackers. Her body was very insistent. 'I need...' She paused, thought. She *was* a little hungry, now the churning had stopped. 'Hang on.' She pushed herself to her feet and walked over to the stone pantry.

Polly opened the door that led to the old-fashioned, walk-in cold room and looked at the shelves that lined the walls, at the marble meat shelf at the far end.

'I know they're here somewhere. I saw them just the other day. I would never buy them. They must be Raff's, vile things. Aha!' Her hand closed triumphantly on a cardboard box. 'Got you.'

She hauled her prize triumphantly out, grabbing a bowl off the oak dresser and setting them both onto the counter. 'Cornflakes! Now I need sugar, lots of sugar. And milk, cold, rich milk. I never usually crave milk.' She pushed the thought away. 'Must be the bug. Maybe I need calcium?'

Raff hadn't said a word, just watched, eyes narrowed, as Polly poured a gigantic bowl of cornflakes, sprinkled them liberally with sugar and added almost a pint of milk to the already brimming bowl. 'This looks amazing,' she told him, almost purring with contentment.

'That looks disgusting. Like something my sister would eat when she's pregnant.'

The word hung there, echoing around the room. Polly put her spoon down and stared at him.

'It's just a bug.' But her voice was wobbling.

'Of course.' He sounded unsure, almost embarrassed, the accent thickening.

'Mixed with jet lag.'

'I know.'
'I'm not…'
'I didn't mean to infer that you were. I'm sorry.'
'But…what if I *am*?'

CHAPTER FOUR

WAS SHE? COULD she be? It should be impossible. It was impossible! Only technically…

Only technically it wasn't.

'Oh no,' she whispered. She looked up at Gabe. He was leaning against the kitchen counter, his face inscrutable. 'It was only once.'

His mouth twisted. 'That's all it takes, *ma chérie*.'

'How could I have been so stupid? What was I thinking?' She pushed the bowl of cornflakes back across the counter. They were rapidly going soggy and her nausea rose again at their mushy state. 'Obviously I wasn't thinking. I was trying not to, that was the point.'

But she had to think now; there was no point in giving into the rising panic swelling inside her. Her throat might be closing up in fear, her palms damp but she could override her body's signals. If only she'd done that ten weeks ago…

Ten weeks! And she hadn't even suspected, putting the nausea and the tiredness down to stress, jet lag, a bug.

It could still be! Two and two didn't always make four did it? Not in some obscure pure mathematical plane. Probably.

'I need a test.'

'Oui.' He was still expressionless. 'In the morning I'll…'

'Not in the morning!' Was he crazy? Did he think she was going to sit around and wait all night when liberation could be just around the corner? 'There's a twenty-four-hour supermarket in Dartingdon, I'll get one from there.'

She was on her feet as she said it. Thank goodness for modern twenty-four-seven life.

'You can't drive.'

She stopped still, swivelled and stared. 'I already said I didn't drink anything.'

'No.' He shook his head. 'But you're in shock. It isn't safe.'

So her hands were shaking a little, her legs slightly weak. She'd be fine. She'd driven the route a thousand times.

'And what if you throw up again?'

'Then I'll pull over. You don't have to take care of me, Gabe. I was big enough to get myself into this mess, I am certainly capable of sorting it out. I don't need anyone.'

His eyes bored into hers. 'If that's true then how did this happen?'

Ouch! That was well and truly below the belt. 'Want me to draw you a diagram?' She could hear the tremor of anger running through her voice and tried to rein it back.

'You fell out with your family here, went to find yourself, felt lost and lonely and so you what? Fell for the first smile and compliment?'

Polly stood stock-still, ice-cold anger running through her veins, her bones, every nerve and sinew. How dared he?

How dared he be so right?

'That wasn't what happened. Not that it has anything to do with you.' Shaking with a toxic mixture of righteous anger, adrenaline and nausea, she marched over to the counter to grab her car keys but before her hand could close on the fob it was whisked away in a decisive masculine hand.

'I'll go.'

'We drive on the left here. And do you even

know where Dartingdon is?' she added slightly lamely. Polly wanted to prove a point but part of her knew he was right. Annoyingly. She was barely fit to run a bath let alone drive twisty country roads.

'I'm a big boy. I'll figure it out.'

'No.' All the anger had drained. Now she was just weary, utterly, achingly tired. 'You can drive but I'll navigate. And I'll scream if you take my beloved car even one centimetre over onto the wrong side.'

He regarded her levelly then nodded. 'Okay. I still think you would be better staying here.'

But she was adamant. Polly had never waited for things to be brought to her—she'd never have made it this far if she had. 'I can't wait that long,' she admitted. 'I need to know straight away.'

'And then what?'

That was the million-dollar question. 'Then I can plan. Everything's better with a plan.'

She was quiet. So quiet Gabe would almost swear that she was asleep except when he glanced over he could see the glare of her phone illuminating the whites of her eyes.

'Concentrate on the road,' she snapped but he could sense the worry under the anger. He had got used to that, with Marie. In the end when the pain had got too much, as the fear and anger and sheer bloody unfairness had overtaken her she had been cross all the time, barely able to be civil, even to those she loved.

Especially to those she loved.

'I am,' he said. He couldn't resist one little provocative grenade. 'If you drove a proper car...'

'This is a proper car!'

'It's a grown-up's toy,' he teased. It actually handled pretty well, the small body taking the many twists and turns of the Oxfordshire country roads surprisingly well. 'Shame you'll have to get rid of it.'

He could feel her stiffen beside him. 'What do you mean?'

'It's a two-seater...' He didn't have to say any more. From the intake of breath he knew his point had hit home.

'Possibly not. We'll know soon enough.' But there wasn't any hope in her voice.

She didn't say anything for the next few miles. Despite his confidence earlier, this was the first time Gabe had actually driven a left-hand drive and it required most of his concentration to stay on the correct side of the road as he navigated the narrow curves. He wasn't helped by the car; low slung and powerful, she was absurdly responsive to his slightest touch, almost as if she were desperate to speed on.

Although there were no street lights in this country corner it wasn't too hard to see his way as he drove through hedge-lined lanes, fields almost at their ripest stretching out on both sides towards gently rolling hills. The summer solstice was nearly upon them and it was barely dark out, more of a gloomy dull grey. Like his mood.

There was no reason for him to feel so…so what? Slighted? Gabe sighed; he really needed to get over himself. One kiss did not equal any kind of relationship.

And if it did he would be headed the other way, right back to France.

It was just, if Polly Rafferty had really indulged in a night of meaningless, no-holds-barred, anonymous sex he wished she'd indulged with him.

He could be wrong, she might often go out prowling bars and clubs for one-night stands but he would bet the oldest bottle of wine in the vine-yard's formidably stocked cellars that this had been a one-off occasion. And pregnant or not she was unlikely to indulge again.

'This doesn't have to change anything. It *doesn't* change anything.' Her voice penetrated his thoughts. Gabe risked a glance across at his reluctant passenger. Polly had pulled herself upright and was looking straight ahead, her jaw firmly set. 'The timing is awful but I could make it work.'

'Didn't you want children?'

There was another long pause. 'I don't *know* children,' she said after a while. 'I don't know how families work, normal ones. Raff and I were raised by our grandparents and they sent us away to school when we were small. It's not something I've ever thought about.' She huffed out a small laugh. 'Not every woman hits thirty and starts counting down her biological clock, you know.'

'But your house, it's begging for a family.' Five bedrooms, the large garden full of hidden corners and climbable trees. Despite the low ceilings and homely furnishings it felt too big, too echoey for just two people. And she had been living there alone for three years.

'It's just a building.' Her voice was dismissive.

Gabe shrugged. He was no psychologist but he had been through enough counselling—support groups, family therapy, grief counselling, chronic illness groups—to know a little bit about the subconscious. The cottage was a family-home wish come true.

'If you say so.'

She shifted, turned to look at him. 'How about you? Dreams of *petits enfants* clustering around your knee one day?'

'I'm a good uncle,' he said shortly.

'Guys can say that, can't they? No pressure to settle down, get married, churn out kids. You have all the time in the world.'

'None of us know how much time we have.' He meant to say it lightly but the words came out too quick, too bitter. He shot her a quick glance. 'I had cancer in my teens, a lymphoma. It teaches you to take nothing for granted.'

Polly gasped, a loud audible intake of breath as she put her hand to her mouth. 'Oh, Gabe. I am so sorry. I didn't mean…'

'It's fine.' This was why he hated people knowing. A brush with mortality and they never treated you the same way again. It was as if you were tainted with the mark of Death's scythe, a constant reminder that no one was safe.

'Besides, I can't.' The words were out before he knew it, the darkness beginning to shadow the car giving it the seal of a confessional, somewhere safe.

'Can't what?'

'Have children. Probably. Chemotherapy, stem-cell treatment...' His voice trailed off; he didn't need to add the rest.

'Oh.' Understanding dawned in the long drawn-out syllable. 'Didn't they freeze any?' Her hand was back over her mouth. 'I'm sorry. I didn't mean to intrude.'

'They didn't think it would have any long-term effects.' He smiled wryly. 'I was seventeen. To be honest it was the last thing I was thinking about—or my parents thought about. But it took longer, needed stronger drugs than they expected. It's okay. I'd rather be healthy.'

Her hand had crept to her stomach. 'Of course.'

'They did say it can change in time but I have never been tested. There's no point. I don't want them anyway,' he surprised himself by offering.

'The worst part of being ill was seeing my parents suffer. I'm not sure I'm strong enough to put myself through that.'

'I watched my father die.' Her voice was flat. 'That wasn't much fun either.'

They didn't speak the rest of the way there. Gabe was too absorbed in his thoughts and Polly had returned to jabbing furiously at her phone as if it could give her all the answers she needed.

Following the signs, he navigated his way around the roundabouts that ringed the old town, pulling off into an ugly development of warehouses and cavernous shops.

'We're here,' he said.

Polly didn't move, just looked out of the window at the neon orange streetlamps and the parking signs. 'Okay.'

'Why don't I go for you?' he suggested but she was already shaking her head.

'Thank you but I really need to do this by myself.'

'Are you sure you have enough?'

Polly bit her lip. Maybe two each of five different brands was slightly excessive but she had to make sure. If Gabe was potentially harbouring an alien life form inside him he would want to know one hundred per cent too.

'No.' She twisted the bag nervously. 'Do you think I should have got three of each?'

'I think you should leave at least one test on the shelves, just in case someone else is tearing through the night in need of answers.'

'Let's just get home.' She tugged impatiently at the car door, glaring at Gabe as he made no move to unlock it.

'Are you sure?'

She stared at him. 'What? You want to pop out for a nice meal first? Maybe go for a moonlight stroll? Of course I'm sure.'

He didn't react. 'I meant maybe you wanted to take the test now. Find out one way or another.'

'Oh.' How had he guessed?

Polly looked around the car park. There were several chain restaurants but they were all showing signs of closing for the night. Or the supermarket toilets; they would still be open.

She bit back a hysterical giggle. She had never actually imagined taking a pregnancy test, let alone taking it in the strip-lit anonymity of a supermarket loo. It wasn't the cosy scene depicted in the adverts.

But then she wasn't the hopeful woman on the advert either.

'There's nowhere here.'

'Not here exactly.' Finally he clicked the button and the doors unlocked. 'We can find somewhere a little more salubrious than this.'

It took him less than five minutes to exit the car park and start back round the ring road, retracing their earlier route.

'Don't worry,' he said as Polly looked worriedly at the sign pointing the way back to Hopeford. 'I've got an idea.'

'I trust you.' And she did. Maybe because she had nobody else—not even herself.

At the Hopeford roundabout Gabe took a different exit, driving into the car park of a large redbrick building. Polly must have driven past it dozens of times but had never registered it before. Why would she? Anonymous roadside hotels offering business deals and cheap weddings weren't her usual style.

'Wait here.' He was gone before she could formulate a reply. Resentment rose up inside her.

Who was he to tell her what to do? She half rose out of her seat, determined to follow him, to regain control.

But no, she reminded herself, she had relinquished control, tonight at least. Polly sank back into her seat and tried to control the panicked race of her heart.

The bag was on her lap, the sharp edges of the boxes an uncomfortable fit against her thighs. Pulling out a handful, Polly turned them this way and that, reading the fine print on them curiously. Fancy being thirty-one and never having even properly seen a pregnancy test before!

But why would she have? She had been good to study with but she had never been the kind of friend others turned to. Not for panicked confidences and surreptitious tests in the school bathrooms or university toilets.

And she had never been the type to slip up herself. Not careful Polly Rafferty.

Not until now.

How could she have not known? Suspected that the bug she just couldn't shift might be something more? But she had continued with the pills her doctor had prescribed her for her trip, relieved to be spared the inconvenience of her monthly cycle, and missed nature's most glaring warning.

'Okay,' she muttered. How hard could taking one of these be? A blue line, two pink lines, a cross for yes. A positive sign? That was a little presumptuous. Another simply said 'pregnant'. She swallowed, hard, the lump in her throat making the simple act difficult. Painful.

She jumped as a knock sounded on her window, muttering as the packets fell to the floor. She hastily gathered them up. They felt wrong, like contraband. It was as if just being seen with them branded her in some unwanted way.

Looking up, she saw Gabe. He must have seen her reading the packets. Heat flooded through her and she took a deep breath, trying her best to summon her usual poise.

She opened the door. 'Hi.'

'They have a room we can use.' He stood aside as she got out of the car and waited while she gathered the dropped boxes, stuffing them into the carrier bag.

'Won't they wonder why we are checking in so late with no luggage?'

Gabe huffed out a short laugh. 'Polly. They will

think we are illicit lovers looking for a bed for an hour, or travellers realising we need a bed for the night. Or, more likely, they won't think at all. Come on.'

He took the bag from her as if it were nothing, as if it didn't carry the key to her hopes and dreams. To the freedom she had never even appreciated until this moment.

'Come on.' He strode off towards the hotel.

Polly hesitated. Maybe she could wait until she got home after all. In fact maybe she could just wait, wait for this nightmare to be over.

Her hand crept to her abdomen and stayed there. What if? There was only one way to find out.

The hotel lobby was as anonymous as the outside, the floor tiled in a nondescript beige, the walls a coffee colour accented by meaningless abstract prints, the whole set off by fake oak fittings. Gabe led the way confidently past the desk and Polly noted how the receptionists' eyes followed him.

And how their eyes rested on her in jealous appraisal, making her all too aware of her old tracksuit, her lack of make-up. She lifted her head; let them speculate, let them judge.

They walked along a long corridor, doors at regular intervals on either side. 'Aha, *voici*,' Gabe muttered and stopped in front of one of the white wooden doors.

Number twenty-six. Such a random number, bland and meaningless. It didn't feel prophetic.

He opened the door with the key card and stood aside to let Polly enter. Her eyes swept around the room. The main part of the room was taken up by a large double bed made up in white linen with a crimson throw and matching pillows. The same tired abstracts were on the walls of the room; a TV and a sizeable desk completed the simple layout.

The door to her right stood open to reveal a white tiled bathroom.

The bathroom.

Panic whooshed through her and Polly put out a hand to steady herself against the wall. It was time.

What if she was pregnant?

What if she wasn't?

The thought froze her. That was what she wanted. Wasn't it?

'I'm going to order some food. I didn't manage more than a couple of forkfuls of that omelette.

You should eat. What do you want?' Gabe's voice broke through her paralysis like a spoon stirring slowly through thick treacle.

Polly blinked at him, trying to make sense of the words. How could he even think of food at a time like this? 'I'm not hungry.'

'I'm ordering for you anyway. I'm going to have a beer. What do you want to drink?' He flashed a look at the bag on the bed. 'You're going to need a lot of liquid to get through that lot.'

As if the whole episode weren't mortifying enough. Why hadn't they invented tests you breathed on?

Gabe sat down on the bed and kicked off his shoes, one hand reaching for the menu, the other for the TV control. He looked like a man completely happy with his surroundings as he swung his legs onto the bed and reclined.

The bed.

The one and only.

'This is a double room.'

He grinned at her. 'I can see why they made you CEO.'

'You booked us a double?'

'I took the room they had available so that

you—' he cast a speaking glance at the bag next to him '—could get on and do what you have to do. I might as well be comfortable, fed and watered while I wait. Panic not, princess. Your virtue is safe with me.'

Or what was left of it, she silently filled in the rest of the sentence. What was she thinking anyway? She was potentially pregnant, definitely sick, had bags under her eyes big enough for a whole week's worth of groceries and was wearing an old tracksuit, her freshly washed hair pulled back into a knot. Clothes she had put on after puking over her outfit, floor and cloakroom. She wasn't exactly a catch.

To be honest she was surprised Gabe hadn't got them separate rooms, not a double. Anything less sexy than Polly Rafferty right now was hard to imagine.

'Right then.' She took a tremulous step forward, then another, leaning forward and grabbing the bag. 'Let's do this thing.'

He looked up from the menu, his eyes dark with concern. 'Do you want…I mean is there anything I can do?'

'You can hardly pee on a stick for me,' Polly

snapped. She took a breath, her cheeks heating up. Great, she could add scarlet and sweaty to her long list of desirable attributes. 'No, really. I don't think either of us will ever recover if you come in there with me.'

The tiles were cold on her cheek and hands and beginning to chill the rest of her body. She should move, get up.

But getting up was a pretty tall order right now. In fact, Polly wasn't sure she was ever going to move again; she could spend the rest of her life curled up here, right?

Curled up in a foetal position. Now that was pretty damn ironic.

A bang on the hotel room door made her start. But of course, Gabe was there. He would take care of it.

She heard the mumbling of voices and the clink of crockery. If only they would shut up. Quiet was good. The bedroom door swung shut with a re-sounding *thunk*.

Good, peace again.

'Polly.'

Drat the man. If she didn't answer maybe he would go away.

'Polly, your food is here.'

The tiles had gone from cold to numbing. Polly liked numb. It was peaceful.

'Polly, if you don't answer me right now I am going to break down the door.'

He wouldn't, would he?

'Final warning, three, two...'

'Go away.' Was that her voice so clear and strong? She thought it would be croaky with years of misuse. But after all it had only been fifteen minutes since she had shut the door.

It just felt like centuries.

'Polly Rafferty, open the door this instant and come and eat some food.'

She pulled a face in the direction of the door.

'Now!'

Her peace had evaporated. He was evidently not going to give up.

'I'm coming.'

She rolled round and clambered painfully to her feet, hugging herself as the cold from the floor permeated every pore, and walked slowly to the door, twisted the lock and inched the door open. 'Satisfied?'

'I ordered you chips. And bread. Carbs are good for sore stomachs.'

'I thought you only ordered things full of vitamins.'

He didn't answer, just walked away to lift the silver covers off the plates on the desk.

'You're having chips as well?' Wonders would never cease. She'd bet half her trust fund that he would go on an extra run tomorrow and not stop until he had burnt off every calorie and gram of fat.

'I wasn't sure that you would cope with the smell of anything else.'

He hadn't asked about the test, not even with his eyes.

'They're positive.'

A flash of something then; sorrow, a hint of anger but both overshadowed with concern. 'They all agree?'

'I only managed to take six, even after drinking a gallon of water.'

She sank onto the bed. 'Oh, God, positive. What do I do?'

He handed her a plate. 'Tomorrow you plan. But now…now you eat.'

Polly was showing no sign of wanting to leave the hotel room. She had managed to eat a few chips and drink the tea he'd ordered. Now she was lying on the bed seemingly absorbed in the music videos playing on the TV.

But Gabe could tell she wasn't hearing a note.

He put the empty plates out into the corridor and walked back into the room. Polly hadn't moved, not even a centimetre. With one eye on her, as cautious as if she were a feral cat, Gabe sat back onto the bed and stretched out alongside her. Close but not touching.

He put his hands behind his head and stared at the ceiling. The plaster was perfectly smooth, as featureless as the rest of the hotel.

'I can't bake.'

He turned his head to look at her. She was still propped up on the pillows and staring at the TV.

'That's okay.'

'Of course it's not okay. You have to be able to bake. No one cares if a mother has an MBA or an amazing job. It's the cupcakes that count. I can't sew either.'

'No, but you work somewhere full of people who can do both those things so why care?'

She moved slowly until she was propped on her side looking at him. Her eyes were almost navy blue, matching the shadows deepening under them. Her skin pale under the rapidly fading tan. 'I bet your mother can bake and sew.'

'*Oui*, but she doesn't have an MBA.'

She didn't answer, just continued to look at him, her eyes searching his face as if he had all the answers.

'I don't know his surname.'

Cold rage swirled. How could anyone seduce this woman and just walk away? There were women who knew the game, who enjoyed playing, who wanted little more than a night or two. They were the ones you played with. 'We can find him.'

'You think?' The hope in her voice was killing. But then she shook her head. 'I don't see how. All I know is that he's Danish. What a mess. He probably wouldn't want to be involved, but he should know.'

'Who is he?'

'Markus. I met him in Mancora after I finished the Inca trail—he was about my age, recently divorced. A little lost.' She tried for a smile. 'Like me.'

'And I thought this was it, my life here, at Rafferty's, was over, that I needed to start again. I needed to be a new Polly.'

'That's a shame,' he said, keeping his voice level despite every trembling instinct. 'I kind of like the old Polly.'

'Me too,' she whispered as if it were a confession. 'But old Polly had failed. No job, nobody who cared about me. Oh, I dated, had serious relationships but I always walked away. Relationships need compromise, you see. Only what they wanted was for *me* to compromise For *me* to work less hours, to attend *their* work dos. To make the relationship work I had to be less. They could just keep on doing what they were doing.'

'Fools.'

Her mouth curved upwards. 'I thought so. I would leave and move on. But old Polly never learnt. She always went out with successful men, businessmen, suits and chauffeured cars and busy schedules and she always, always failed. So why not try someone new? Someone different?'

That had always been Gabe's philosophy. New, different, meaningless. It didn't sound so pretty on her lips.

'It makes sense.' In a warped way it did. He understood exactly why she had thrown caution to the wind.

'I had a list, of things I had never done, things most people did in their teens and early twenties. Swim naked, sleep under the stars.' She flushed. 'Have sex on a beach.' She shook her head. 'It sounds so childish.'

'No, it doesn't.' Gabe knew what it was like to miss out on things. He hadn't gone to teen parties, hadn't experimented with girls or beer or flirted with danger. Instead he'd hovered on the brink of death, he'd fallen in love, he'd lost everything.

'I've never done any of those things either,' he confided, trying to push away the image of Polly, tall and willowy, tanned bare skin glowing in the moonlight.

'It was supposed to mean nothing. Only now...' Her voice trailed off. 'I've messed up so badly.

I finally have everything I always wanted but I don't know what to do.'

'You don't have to figure it out tonight.' Gabe was supposed to be keeping his distance, supposed to be the chauffeur, nothing more, but watching her tears spill out, hot and heavy, he couldn't not act. Without thought he edged closer, pulled her in, wrapped his arms around her and allowed her body to settle along his.

She fitted like a glove, her head on his shoulder, her chest against his, hip against hip.

'How could I mess up like this? I have never ever put a foot wrong. The one time I allow myself to just act, to not think and it explodes all over my dreams. I need to be a CEO, not a mother.'

'Who says you can't be both? When I was diagnosed I had so many plans. Plans to pull the hottest girl at school, to captain the rugby team. Plans to ace my exams. I had to rethink everything. In the end my plan was to live. And I did.'

'And the other things?' she asked softly.

'I didn't pull the hottest girl in school, but I fell in love with someone much better.' Gabe tightened his grip and tried not to remember Marie crying in his arms. 'I gave up rugby but took up marathons and triathlons—and I still aced my exams. Plans change, they adapt, you'll be fine.'

'How?'

Gabe sighed. It took time, adjustment, pain— but she wasn't ready to hear that. Not yet. 'We can figure it out tomorrow. It's all going to be okay. I promise, it's going to be okay.'

CHAPTER FIVE

IT WAS WARM, the mattress firm and comfortable but not quite as firm and comfortable as the bare chest she was nestled against. Polly sighed and rolled in a little closer, allowing her hand to slip round the firm midriff to trail along the smooth back.

Hang on. Skin? Muscle?

She snatched her hand back and rolled away, swallowing back the all too familiar nausea that hit her the moment she moved. And with it reality came crashing through the sleep fog, harsh, bitter. Terrifying.

She lay there trying to summon up enough strength to move, and doing her best to ignore the almost overwhelming temptation to move closer to Gabe, to put her arm back around him, snuggle in close and go back to sleep.

Getting into bed with strange men had got

her into this situation. It looked as if she hadn't learned anything!

Not that the two cases were at all the same. She was still fully dressed in the tracksuit she had thrown on last night.

She was still pregnant.

An ache began to throb, squeezing the side of her temples, the sticky soreness of her eyes an unwelcome reminder of the tears she had shed the night before. The weakness she had displayed.

Polly put her hand over her mouth, stifling the groan that threatened to escape. What had she done? She had *cried*. Cried in front of Gabriel Beaufils of all people. She had just handed him the keys to utter humiliation. How could she spin this situation as a positive thing when he could expose her any second? Tell everyone that she had messed up.

That she was fallible.

But would he? Heat burned her cheeks as she remembered his gentleness, his words, his confidences.

No, somehow Polly knew deep down that he wouldn't expose her. But he would still *know*.

Know that she wasn't strong, that she had allowed herself to lean on him.

It couldn't happen again.

'Morning.'

Polly turned her head slowly. Gabe was propped up on one elbow facing her. His expression was warm, radiating concern. Concern that she didn't need or want.

Polly slowly pulled herself up to a seating position, glad that the nausea seemed to have abated after that first rush.

'I thought we had a deal,' she said.

'A deal?' He looked surprised.

'That you were going to keep your shirt on.'

A slow appreciative smile spread over his face. It wasn't fair, Polly thought as the breath hitched in her throat. He already had soulful eyes and a well-cut jawline. Adding a smile that made you want to respond in kind, that sent a jolt of appreciation into the pit of your stomach, gave you a sudden urge to reach out and trace the firm mouth was too much.

'That agreement was only for the office,' he said. 'We are no longer in the office.'

'No.' Polly looked around at the generic bland furnishings. 'We certainly aren't. I'm sorry.'

'No need.'

'There's every need,' she corrected him. 'I dragged you out here. I'm pretty sure this isn't your usual style.'

Gabe's eyes swept over the room, coming to rest on Polly. She fought the urge to fidget, to straighten her mussed hair, pull at her baggy top.

'I don't know,' he said. 'I've had worse evenings.'

Polly stared at him, an unexpected bubble of laughter rising. 'Of course you have,' she said. 'What's more fun than a little vomit, a crazy late-night car ride and a night with a weeping woman in a downmarket hotel?'

'It was more than a little vomit. How are you feeling?'

Polly put a hand to her stomach, allowing it to linger there for a moment. Somewhere in there was the beginning of new life. A life she had created.

'Better,' she said, surprised that it was true. She thought for a moment, savouring the hollow feeling that had miraculously appeared. 'Hungry. Really hungry.'

'Room service?'

Polly shook her head. 'I need to get out,' she said. 'Although...' she looked at herself '...I'm not really fit to be seen.' But she didn't want to go home yet.

'How hungry are you?'

She was grateful that he didn't insult her intelligence by telling her that she looked fine. She had eyes and she still had the tattered remnants of her pride.

'Why?'

'If you can wait half an hour,' he suggested, 'I'll pop back to that supermarket and pick up a toothbrush and hairbrush and anything else you need. Then I think we should go out for the day.'

'Go out?' Polly leant back and eyed him suspiciously. 'To do what? We have papers to write, remember?'

'We've both put in a ridiculous amount of hours this week.' Gabe rolled off the bed unperturbed and picked up his T-shirt from the floor, shaking it out fastidiously before putting it back on. 'And it was an emotional evening.' He smiled across at her as he said it, taking any possible sting out of the words. 'I need a walk, some fresh air and a change of scenery. Are you in?'

A vision of her laptop floated into Polly's mind. The half-written report. The statistics and recommendations and examples. The spreadsheet full of costings and projections and risk analysis. 'I should work,' she said, pulling her hair out of its ponytail and running her fingers through the tangled lengths.

Gabe didn't say anything, just regarded her levelly. Polly glared back.

'Last chance.'

She should work. She'd just had three months off, for goodness' sake. So what if she felt as if a steamroller had run her over physically and emotionally before reversing and finishing the job? She wasn't paid to have feelings or problems or illnesses.

She should work.

Polly glanced over at the window. The sun was peeping in around the blinds. Was that birds she could hear singing, their tuneful chirps not quite masked by the roar of passing traffic? She'd spent all of the previous summer indoors, working. The strangest part about travelling had been adjusting to being outdoors, the blissful heat as the sun soaked into her weary bones. She had missed out on so many summery weekends.

And next summer everything would be completely changed. There would be another person to take care of.

She glared at Gabe, who was still waiting, arms folded and an enquiring eyebrow raised.

'Oh, okay then. Let me write you a shopping list.'

Polly spent the entire half-hour of Gabe's absence in the hotel's surprisingly powerful shower, letting the hot jets blast away the kinks in her shoulders and back, beat the tangles out of her hair and massage the worry out of her mind. By the time Gabe rapped softly on the door she felt vaguely human again.

Wrapping the towel tightly around her, she took the proffered carrier bag Gabe handed through the bathroom door. Polly was conscious of an unprecedented intimacy. Gabe had selected her clothes, underwear, her shoes.

It was disconcerting, made her feel vulnerable.

Which was ridiculous; she often ordered outfits or lingerie when she needed a quick change for an unexpected meeting or lunch. They were picked out and delivered by any one of the many anonymous salesmen or women she employed and she never felt a moment's hesitation about wearing things they had handled.

She didn't even pick her own toothpaste; her concierge service took care of all her household purchases.

But Polly couldn't help staring at the pretty lilac bra and pants, the sleeveless, fifties-style summer dress in a vibrant blue, the flared skirt ending just before her knees. Had he just grabbed the first things he had seen—or were they chosen especially for her?

Either way it was a choice between the dress or the tracksuit she'd slept in.

Slowly Polly slipped on the underwear and buttoned up the dress, her hands uncharacteristically clumsy. They fitted perfectly. Her figure was unchanged—for now.

Luckily she always carried a selection of miniatures from her favourite make-up brands with her and in just a few minutes she was ready, tinted moisturiser hiding the last of the damage from the evening's tears, mascara and some lip gloss an armour to help her through the day. Slipping her feet into the flowered flip-flops Gabe had provided, she stepped out of the bathroom strangely shy.

'Better?' she asked.

'That colour suits you. I thought it would.' There was a huskiness in his voice that reached deep inside her and tugged, a sweet sensual pull that made her sway towards him.

'Matches my eyes,' she said, aware what a lame comment it was but needing to say something, to try and break the hypnotic spell his words had cast.

'*Non.*' Gabe was still staring at her as if she were something deliciously edible. 'Your eyes are darker.'

Polly felt exposed before the hunger in his eyes. The dip of the dress suddenly seemed horribly low-cut, the hemline indecently short, her arms too bare. 'I've never worn a supermarket dress before,' she said.

'No.' He gave a quick bark of laughter and just like that the air of sensuality that had been swelling, filling the room, disappeared. 'Polly Rafferty in prêt-à-porter. There's a first for everything.'

'I wear ready-to-wear all the time,' she protested.

'Designer diffusion ranges?' He laughed again as she nodded. 'What about while you were away?'

'It pays to buy quality. It lasts longer,' she told him, unwilling to admit that even her travelling sarong had cost more than the entire outfit she was currently wearing. 'Now, I believe you promised me breakfast and then we need to decide what we're going to do.'

'We could just drive and see where we end up,' Gabe suggested.

'Oh, no, if I am taking a day off it needs to be well planned so I make the most of it,' Polly told him. 'And if you think I'm letting you drive my car one more time you're crazy. My nerves won't take the strain.'

Gabe grinned. 'We'll see,' was all he said. 'Come on, Polly. Let's go and organise a day of spontaneous fun.'

Of course it had begun to rain. Why had he given up the golden beaches of California or the flower-strewn meadows of his home for this grey, drizzly island?

Although Paris could be rainy too, Gabe conceded. But somehow in Paris even the rain had a certain style. In the English countryside it was just wet.

'Thoughts, Mr Spontaneity?'

Gabe sat back in his seat and considered. The prospects weren't appealing: a walk, a tour round a stately home, a visit to yet another of the exquisite market towns where the old houses were built from the golden stone with which the region abounded. If they were going to do that they might as well return to Hopeford—the most exquisite and golden and historic of the lot.

The sea? But they were in the middle of the country and the nearest coast was over one hundred miles away.

He could, if he hadn't been overcome with a ridiculous chivalry, have been on a train into the city right now. A visit to the gym, a couple of hours in the office and then a few beers in Kensington with some other émigrés. But there had been something vulnerable about the elegant Polly Rafferty slumped on a cheap hotel bed, that golden hair piled up into an untidy ponytail, red-eyed, white-faced. The circumstances couldn't have been more different, the women more different, but for one heart-stopping moment she had reminded him of Marie.

Of Marie as she began to give up.

The irony was that he had spent the last ten years turning away from women who provoked even the smallest reminder of his ex. One hint of vulnerability, of neediness and he was gone—so why was he sitting here watching the rain lash the windscreen on a magical mystery tour to nowhere?

Was it because he respected Polly? Knew that once she adjusted she would pick herself up and walk tall, head high, daring anyone to criticise her choices?

Or because he instinctively knew that she hid her weaknesses from the world. He might have been in the right place at the right time—or the wrong place at the wrong time—for her to collapse on him the way she had.

No matter why his usual 'turn tail and run' instincts weren't functioning normally. Not yet.

But they would. He didn't have to worry.

'What do you want to do?' He turned the question onto her.

'Not get wet?' Polly glared at the windscreen as if she could stop the rain with pure force of will. 'I took the day off to enjoy the sunshine. Besides, my new outfit doesn't include a cardigan or an umbrella.'

'It was warm just an hour ago. I forgot to factor in the crazy British weather.'

'Between May and September it's wise to carry an umbrella, a wrap and sunscreen at all times. Let that be your first lesson in British life. That and always have an indoor alternative.'

'I would suggest lunch but after that breakfast you just ate...' he said slyly.

'I'm eating for two!' The colour rose high in her cheeks. 'And I've barely eaten anything for the last week or two. I was in a major calorie deficit. Hang on, what does that sign say?'

Gabe peered through the slanting rain at the colourful poster, gamely flapping in the wet and cold. 'Probably some kind of fete,' he said. 'The British summer, always wet and cold and yet full of outdoor events. You're an optimistic isle, I'll give you that. Or crazy,' he added thoughtfully.

'No, it's not that. Oh!' With that squeal she put the indicator on and turned down the winding lane indicated by the poster. 'It's a Vintage Festival. Do you mind?'

'As long as it's dry and indoors.'

'What? Mr Triathlete scared of a little rain?'

'*Non*, just a man from the South of France who likes summer to be just that, summery.'

'Oh, boy, are you in the wrong country.'

The small country lane was long and winding and it took Polly a few moments to navigate its twists and turns before she followed another sign that took them through wrought-iron gates and up a sweeping, tree-lined driveway. Gabe caught a glimpse of large, graceful house before the road took them round to a busy car park.

'Wow.' Polly's voice was full of envy as she pulled to a stop, her eyes eagerly looking around. 'People have come in style.'

Hers was by no means the only modern car there but even her sporty two-seater was put firmly in the shade by the array of well-loved vintage cars from all eras. 'If I'd known we were coming I'd have brought Raff's Porsche,' Polly said sadly.

'It's a seventies car so not really vintage but older than this.'

The look she gave her own car was scathing, which, Gabe thought, was a little rich considering the fuss she had made over him driving it the night before.

'Aren't they gorgeous?' She had jumped out of the car, heedless of the rain, which had lightened to a drizzle, and was trailing her hand over a cream Austin Healey. 'And look at that Morris Minor, it's pristine. Wow, what great condition. Somebody loves you, don't they, baby?' she crooned.

Crooned. To a car. To an *old* car.

'They are very nice,' Gabe said politely as he joined her. 'For old cars.'

'Shh!' Polly threw him a scathing glance. 'They'll hear you. Don't listen to the nasty man,' she told the Austin consolingly. 'He's French.'

'We have old cars in France too,' Gabe said indignantly, stung by the slur to his country. 'I just prefer mine new.'

She patted his arm consolingly. 'This might not be the right place for you. Come on.'

It was a new side to Polly. Excited, eager, playful. It was a side he bet her staff never saw, that barely anybody saw.

'So, where are we?' Gabe asked as they walked along the chipping-strewn path that took them through a small wooded area and towards the house. Bunting was strung along the path, dripping wet yet defiantly cheerful.

'Geographically I'm not entirely sure, socially we're at a vintage festival.'

Clear as mud. 'Which is?'

Polly stopped and turned. 'Surely people go to them in France?'

'Possibly,' he said imperturbably. 'I, however, have not.'

'You are in for such a treat,' she said, grabbing his arm and pulling him along. 'There's usually stalls where you can buy anything old: clothes, furniture, jewellery. And tea and cakes, and makeovers and dancing. Loads of people come all dressed up in their favourite decade, mostly forties and fifties but you do get twenties and sixties as well.'

Gabe looked at her curiously. 'Do you go to these a lot?'

Her face fell. 'Not any more,' she said. 'Which

is a shame because there are loads now, big affairs like this one looks to be. But I did go to a few vintage clubs and smaller affairs when I was at university. I've always loved the twenties; you know, flappers and jazz and the art deco style. Everything that was around when Rafferty's was founded.'

'Why don't you go any more?'

She sighed. 'The usual,' she said. 'Time—or lack of. I used to collect nineteen twenties accessories; costume jewellery, compacts, that kind of thing, but I haven't even wandered into an antique shop for a couple of years. Ooh.' Her face lit up. 'This is great timing. We could have a vintage pop-up at Rafferty's? Our centenary is in just a few years. We could have a whole series of twenties-inspired events leading up to that?'

Gabe had no intention of still being there in a few years but he could picture it perfectly. 'Is this just so you can dress up as a flapper?'

'Of course.' She looked down at her outfit. 'Although today I am loosely channelling the fifties. You must have known we were coming here when you picked out the dress.'

Gabe could see the house clearly now; they had

ended up at a stately home after all. But this was
a place gone back in time, to the middle of the
last century if not back to its seventeenth-century
roots.

The path had brought them out onto a large terrace at the back of the house overlooking lawns
and ornamental gardens that seamlessly seemed
to merge into the fields beyond. The furthest lawn
was covered with an array of carnival rides, none
of which was younger than Gabe, horses going
round and round in a never-ending circle, helter-
skelters and coconut shies.

Tables and chairs were dotted all around the terrace and lawns, served by a selection of vintage
ice-cream vans parked in a row by the entrance
gate, some selling the eponymous food, others
cream teas, cakes or drinks.

'It's beautiful,' Polly breathed, still hanging onto
his arm, her gaze transfixed on the scene before
them. 'Doesn't everyone look fabulous? We're
completely underdressed, especially you!'

Swing music was coming from the house,
clearly audible through the parade of open doors.
Parading in and out were people from another
era: brightly lipsticked women with elaborate hair

accompanied by men in old-fashioned military uniforms. Behind them girls with big skirts and ponytails were chatting to men with Brylcreemed hair and attitude to match. It was all pretty cool— if you were into fancy dress.

It had never been Gabe's kind of thing. Life was a mystery as it was; why complicate it by pretending to be someone you weren't? By emulating the lives of those long gone?

'It's a good thing the rain's stopped.'

Polly huffed. 'And people say the English are obsessed with the weather. Come on, Gabe. Let's go in.'

'What do you think?' Polly twirled around in front of Gabe, She hadn't been able to resist the opportunity to have her hair pin-curled and it hadn't taken much to persuade her into the accompanying makeover.

Or a new outfit. 'You look like you're from a film,' he said. Polly wasn't sure whether he meant it as a compliment or not but decided to go with it.

'That's the idea.' She looked down at the pink-flowered silk tea dress. 'It's not twenties but it will do. You need something too. A coat. Or a hat! We should get you a hat. This is so much fun. Why haven't I done this for so long?'

She led the protesting Gabe over to a stall specialising in military overcoats. 'I hope they have a French coat,' she said. 'Army, air force or navy?'

She knew she was chattering a bit too much, was being a little too impulsive, happily trying—and buying—anything that took her fancy.

It was better than thinking or worrying. She was almost fooling herself that everything was okay, that nothing had changed.

She wasn't fooling Gabe though. She could see it in his eyes.

'Lighten up.' She held a coat up against him. 'You're the one who wanted a day out, a change of scenery, remember?'

'Oui.' But his smile seemed forced, concern still radiating from him. Concern for her.

Unwanted, unneeded.

Suddenly the dress seemed shabby rather than chic, the lipstick heavy on her mouth. She had just wanted a day to forget about everything, a day with no responsibilities or decisions.

'I need some air.' She pushed past him, ignoring his surprised exclamation.

The swing band was still going strong in the ballroom and couples were engaging in gymnastics on the dance floor, a series of complicated lifts and kicks. At any other time Polly would have stopped to watch, to join in with the onlookers enthusiastically applauding each daring move, but she felt stifled, too hot, too enclosed. She wandered over to the terrace, stopping at one of the ice-cream vans to buy a sparkling water and took it over to a table where she examined her impulse purchases.

They were a mixed bag. A few old crime novels, a rather lovely, shell-shaped compact still with the wrist chain attached, two rose-covered side plates and a matching cake stand and some bunting made out of old dress material. It might look nice in the baby's room, she thought idly.

The baby's room.

Her breath whooshed out of her body and she held onto the iron table, glad of the cold metal beneath her palm, anchoring her to the world. She was pregnant. That was her reality and no amount of impromptu days out could change that.

But the expected panic, the gnawing pain in her stomach didn't materialise. Instead she felt light;

it was okay. She didn't have a plan or any idea what to do next but it was okay.

For what must be the hundredth time that week Polly put her hand on her stomach but not in illness, or shock, or horror.

'Hello,' she whispered.

Nobody answered, there was no resulting flutter or any acknowledgement of her words, yet everything had changed.

She wasn't going to be alone any more.

'Would you like an ice cream?'

Polly pulled her hand away as if she had been caught doing something wrong.

'I'm okay,' she began, but the words died on her lips. 'What are you wearing?'

'They didn't have any French coats,' he said. 'So I got a hat instead.'

The trilby should have looked incongruous with the jeans and T-shirt, but somehow he made it look edgy.

Disturbingly sexy.

'It suits you.'

'What have you got there?' Gabe nodded at the bags spread over the table.

'Bits and bobs, bunting.' She looked up, met his eyes. 'For the baby's room.'

He tipped the trilby back; the gesture made him look almost heartbreakingly young, like a World War Two pilot heading back to base for a final mission.

'I hope he likes flowers, then,' he said doubtfully.

Polly gathered the bunting back up, stuffing it into the bag. 'He might be a she, and either way no child of mine will be constrained by gender constructs.' She was aware that she sounded stuffy and that laughter was lurking in his watchful dark eyes.

For a moment she had a view of another path. One where the man teasing her wasn't a momentary diversion in her journey. One where the baby wasn't a shock to deal with but a welcome and much anticipated event.

A world where she might bicker playfully over the suitability of floral bunting, the colour of the paint, where to put the cot and the name of the first teddy bear. Where she wouldn't be doing this alone.

'So do you?' Gabe broke in on her thoughts.

She blinked, confused. Did she what? Want to take a different path? It was a little late for that.

'Polly? Ice cream?'

'Oh. No, no thank you. Actually, I think I want a walk. The grounds look spectacular.' Walk away from her thoughts and the sudden, unwanted regrets.

Gabe cast a doubtful look at the sky. 'Those clouds are pretty dark.'

Rolling her eyes, Polly got up and picked up her bags. 'You have a hat to keep you dry. Honestly, Gabe, you're not going to last five minutes in England if you can't cope with a bit of rain.'

'A bit? Not a problem. This nasty drizzle...' his accent elongated the word contemptuously '...it's not natural. I can't understand why the Normans didn't just turn straight around and go home as soon as they landed and saw the sky.'

'Exactly.' Polly began to walk away from the house, across the wet lawns and towards a small path covered in wood chippings that led through the cluster of trees. 'Romans, Vikings, Normans—rainy or not we're still quite the prize.'

Apart from a disbelieving snort Gabe didn't reply and they walked towards the woods in a companionable silence. After a moment Gabe reached across and took the carrier bags from her. Polly froze for a moment and then loosened her fingers and allowed him to relieve her of her load.

They wandered along for a few more moments, the air heavy with the promise of summer rain. Polly inhaled, enjoying the freshness of the countryside; the heady scent of wet leaves mixed with the damp earth and sawdust from the path.

They rounded a corner and the trees came to an abrupt end; in front of them a pretty ornamental lake stretched ahead, the path skirting the edge.

'Okay, Mr Spontaneity, right or left?'

'What is that?' Gabe sounded startled. 'Have we stumbled onto the set of a horror film?'

Polly followed his disbelieving gaze and saw a dark grey stone tower perched on the edge of the lake, the jagged edge of the spire reaching up into the sky.

'It's a folly. You know...' as he looked at her in query '...a couple of centuries ago it was the craze to build some kind of gothic ruin in a picturesque place. Around the time you were chopping aristocrats' heads off.'

'This is exactly why we were chopping off

heads, if they squandered money on such crazy projects.'

'Hence the name. Want to take a look? There might be a princess for you to rescue at the top, or a prince in need of my knightly skills.'

It only took a few minutes to reach the base of the tower and Polly stood on tiptoe trying to get a look inside but the narrow slits that passed for ground-floor windows were set too high. 'Where's the door?'

Gabe had wandered off around to the other side. 'Here. Are you sure you want to risk it? You might disappear, never to be seen again, kidnapped to be the bride of a headless horseman.'

Polly joined him by the heavy oak door, the hinges exaggerated iron studs. 'Is it locked?'

'Only one way to find out.' Gabe grasped the heavy iron ring and turned it and, with a creak so loud Polly jumped, the door swung open.

'Ready? It looks dark in there.'

'So *you* are scared of ghosts?' she teased.

'*Non*, not ghosts. Spiders and rats on the other hand I am not so keen on.'

Rats? Polly shuddered, an involuntary movement of complete horror. She edged back. 'You think there are rats?'

'Hundreds. And cockroaches too,' he added helpfully.

Polly glared at him. 'Move aside, I'm going in.'

With an exaggerated bow Gabe stood aside, allowing her to precede him into the room.

'There are no stairs, how disappointing. Definitely no stranded royalty for us to rescue.' Polly swivelled slowly, taking in the large circular room paved in grey flagstones, the steep sides rising all the way up to the pointed tip of the tower. There were no other floors but it was mercifully dry. And free of any evidence of rat infestations.

'I still don't understand. What is it for?' Gabe had followed her in.

Polly flung her arms open as she turned. 'Probably somewhere for illicit trysts.'

'Ah, for the nobleman to meet the maid.' He leant back against the wall of the tower, arms crossed, face full of amusement, the hat still tilted back on his head giving him a rakish air.

Polly tilted her chin and stared up at the windows and considered. 'Or for the lady of the house to meet the gamekeeper. Or maybe the stable boy.'

She looked across at Gabe to share the joke but he had gone still, his gaze focused intently on Polly. 'Is that what you would have done? Snuck out to meet the gamekeeper?'

Polly felt a jolt of heat hit the pit of her stomach as their eyes snagged and held, a flash of that first, unacknowledged attraction zipping between them.

'Or the stable boy.' Was that her voice? So husky.

'Of course. What would you have done with the stable boy in this room far away from everyone and everything?' His eyes were so dark, so intense it was hard to look into them, not to be swallowed up in their depths. Polly dropped her gaze to his mouth. Remembered how sure it had been. How demanding.

The heat spread.

'I don't know,' she lied, her mind filled with irresistible images of Gabe, those long legs clad in breeches, a shirt open at the neck. Her mouth dried. She could feel the heat of his gaze, scorching her where she stood, her whole body burning where it fell upon her.

But she couldn't move, desire humming deep in her veins, thrilling to the caress of his eyes.

'Non?' He pushed off the wall, walking towards

her with sure, graceful strides. 'You came here to talk? To touch?' He raised one hand to her face, sliding a finger down her cheek, the lightest of embraces.

'Maybe,' she whispered.

The memory of their earlier kiss was throbbing through her. She could taste him, feel his arms around hers, the lean strength in his hold, the deftness of his touch. He was so close. She only had to step forward, lean against him, raise her face to his.

The desire pounded harder, her heart beating an insistent drum, every pulse point throbbing with her need to close in. To take the kiss further, explore him.

Just one step.

'What's this?'

'Cool, it's a castle!'

Excitable voices outside as sudden, as shocking as the cold water she had poured on Gabe just a few days ago. As shocking, as sobering. Polly took a step back.

'I think...' She took a breath, tried to get her ragged breathing under control. 'I'm tired. Maybe it's time to go home.'

Home. Sanity. Sense. There might be an undeniable attraction between them but now was not the time to act on it. Not while everything was changing, not while she was so vulnerable.

Polly walked across the room and picked up the bags Gabe had left by the wall. Without looking back she left the tower, and left the moment behind.

CHAPTER SIX

'DO YOU WANT to go over these papers before the meeting?'

Polly sat back in her chair and frowned as Gabe folded his long, lean frame into the chair opposite her desk. 'Now you have your own office it would be polite if you knocked.'

'Of course.' Not that he looked in the slightest bit put out, more amused. 'Do you?'

'Do I what?'

His eyebrows shot up. 'Want to go over the papers, of course. The board meeting *is* this afternoon.'

Oh, yes. That. In just a couple of hours her grandfather, Raff and the rest of the board would be sitting in Rafferty's renowned tearooms being suitably feasted before the meeting began.

She was expected to attend. Polly repressed a sigh. Normally she looked forward to these occasions, the buttering-up of contacts, starting to get her case across to the more swayable board members before the official business began, working out whose vote she could count on.

But today the usual thrill was missing; there was so much at stake; her return, Raff on the Board. Consolidating her position before she announced her news.

'We could have gone over the papers last night,' she pointed out, trying to prevent a waspish note from creeping into her voice.

Of course Gabe was free to do whatever he liked; she wasn't his landlady or wife. But surely it was plain good manners to let her know that he wasn't going to be back that night—or even that week.

Not that it was any of her business where he slept. As long as he looked refreshed, smart and in control for the meeting and was well prepared that was all that mattered. Whatever else he got up to—and who he got up to it with—was of no interest to Polly.

It wasn't jealousy that twisted her stomach as she watched him lean in that inch too close to Cordelia from Lingerie or to Amy from Accounts, those liquid brown eyes fixed soulfully on his unwitting victim, the way he murmured low and sweet. No, it was worry about an HR nightmare begging to happen. It was morning sickness.

'I was working late last night,' he said mildly. 'Some of my best contacts are in the U.S. West Coast so it was long past closing by the time I finished getting the information I needed. It was easier to stay here—sleeping in my own office, you'll be glad to hear.' His smile was fleeting but intimate and Polly's breath hitched in her throat.

Unbidden, a memory of her first sight of him flashed through her mind, the strength in that lean body, the tattoo whose lines and curves haunted her dreams.

'I don't think our insurance covers overnight stays. You should stay in a hotel or get the town car home.' She knew she sounded prim. That was fine; prim was good.

'Yes, ma'am.' Another amused look, as if they were sharing a joke only known to the two of them.

Polly inhaled, long and painful. Her heart *wasn't* picking up speed. For goodness' sake, one night of being held, of having her back rubbed and her hair stroked and she was a mushy wreck. It must be the hormones; the same ones that had her tearing up at life insurance adverts.

'So, are you ready now?' Gabe pulled out his smartphone and a USB stick.

'Ready?'

'To go over the papers,' he said patiently.

'Oh, yes. The papers.'

Yep. Hormones. Mush. And apparently turning her into Echo, which, she thought, looking over at the nonchalant man lounging opposite, made him Narcissus. Her eyes flickered over long legs outstretched, shirt collar unbuttoned, sleeves rolled up and day-old stubble; he looked more like an aftershave model than a Vice CEO.

Well, if the Greek allegory fitted…

Regardless, she was no sappy nymph, wafting around in hope of a smile.

'Are you okay?'

'Fine.' She summoned up as much poise as she could. 'Let's get on with this. We don't have much time.'

He looked at her critically, concern etched onto his face. 'Is it the baby? Do you need to lie down?'

'I'm pregnant, Gabe.' No, the ground didn't open up as she said the words out loud, nor did her grandfather appear in an accusatory puff of smoke. 'I'm not ill.'

If he heard the stiffness in her voice he didn't react, firing more questions at her like tiny, yet intensely irritating arrows pricking away at her conscience. 'Are you eating properly? Have you made a doctor's appointment yet?'

Oh, my goodness. It was like being stuck at a baby shower with no easy way of escape—only this time she hadn't primed Rachel to call her with a prefabricated crisis after twenty minutes as she did every time she couldn't get out of the sickly sweet events. If he even mentioned stretch marks or yoga or stitches then one of them would be headed straight out of the window. And she didn't much care which one it was.

'Look, I really appreciate what you did for me last weekend.' There, she said it quite normally despite her urge to grind the words out through gritted teeth. 'But this really isn't any of your business and I would appreciate it if you just...' She searched for a polite way to tell him to butt out. 'Just don't discuss it any more,' she said a little lamely.

He quirked an eyebrow. 'You seem very stressed, Polly. Have you considered yoga?'

Breathe, breathe again and again. It was no good. 'Butt out, Gabe!'

He put his hands up in surrender but his eyes were laughing. 'I'm sorry. Business first. Of course.'

'Good.' But she was unsettled. What if he was right? Should she see a doctor? It was probably the first thing most women did.

What if her independence hurt the baby? Polly clenched her fists; she wanted to reach down again, to cradle her stomach and make a silent vow to the baby that, unorthodox as its beginnings were, as much of a shock the whole thing was, she would do her best to keep it safe. Do her best to love it. But with those mocking eyes fixed on her she wouldn't allow herself to show any signs of softening.

'Hang on.' She couldn't look at Gabe. It felt like giving in. 'I'm just going to call my GP. I'll be with you as soon as I can'

She looked tired. Pale, drawn and thin. And vulnerable. It was a good thing he was hardened against vulnerable women.

'Thanks, yes. I will.' Her conversation at an end, Polly put down the phone and leant forward until her head touched the desk, her hands clasped in front of her. He could see the breaths shuddering through her. Slowly she straightened, pulling at the pins that held her hair in place, running her hands through the freed strands.

'I'm sorry, Gabe, but I need to go in right now.' She smiled, a brief perfunctory smile that didn't go anywhere near her eyes. 'Perils of being a Rafferty. They like to see us early.'

'Sounds like a benefit to me.' It never ceased to amaze Gabe how those with good health took it for granted. He'd been like that once, heedless of his body and strength, unknowing what a miracle every breath, every step, every sensation was.

'Daddy was so young when he had his stroke, they worry about blood pressure.' She was gathering her papers and phone together to put into her bag. 'I tried to put them off until tomorrow but it was easier just to agree to go in. I know we need to talk about the papers. We'll just have to skip the board lunch.'

'I could come with you. We can talk on the way, better use of both our time.' His suggestion had nothing to do with seeing her reluctance to go, knowing how tough it must be to face so many changes alone.

She stopped dead and stared at him. 'You want to come to the doctor's with me? Why ever would you want to do that? I would have thought you of all people would have had enough of anything medical.'

'I'm not planning to come in with you and hold your hand, just to discuss business on the way.'

'I'm walking,' she said, almost defiantly. 'It's only a mile away and the sun's out. I could do with some fresh air.'

'Air sounds good,' he agreed. 'I missed out on a run yesterday. If you're good I might even buy you a frozen yogurt on the way back.'

Rafferty's was situated in the heart of London, not far from the bustle of Oxford Street, close to the rarefied boutiques of Bond Street. Tourists, commuters, shoppers and workers pounded the pavements in an endless throng of busy chatter and purposeful movement. There were times when Gabe would catch the scent of car exhausts, cigarettes, fried food and perfume and feel such a longing for the flower-filled air of Provence it almost choked him.

And there were times when these crowded streets felt like home. When knowing the short-cuts, the local shops, the alleyways, the cafés and bars off the tourist track, which tube stop was next, when it was quicker to walk was instinct. It gave him a certain satisfaction, a sense of be-longing.

But Polly didn't need to belong. She might have moved to a quiet town miles from the capital but London ran through her veins, was in her blood. It was evident in her confidence, the way she moved through the crowd, never putting a foot out of place, seamlessly blending in.

And yet she'd chosen to leave. The city girl living in a sleepy rural town. The defiantly single woman living in a house made for an old-fash-ioned family with several children and a large golden dog. What was real? Did she even know?

'Do you miss London?'

'I'm here every day.'

'To work, not to play.' He grinned at her, but there was no responsive smile.

She didn't answer for a while. 'Everyone thought

I was crazy when I moved to Hopeford—even though I bought my five-bedroom cottage for the same price as my two-bedroom flat,' she said eventually. 'People in their twenties *come* to London, they don't leave it—they only move out when they have children, or if they want to totally reinvent themselves.'

'People come to London for the same reason,' he said, but so quietly he wasn't sure whether or not she heard him.

'I went to Hopeford on a whim,' she said. She still wasn't looking at him, almost talking to herself. 'It was Sunday. I was working as usual. I lived around here, in a beautiful flat, walking distance to Rafferty's. I worked all the time.'

'You still do.' Not that he could talk. But at least he had his training to break up the days, refresh his brain. Polly lived with her laptop switched on.

'That Sunday I was in by six a.m. I couldn't sleep. And by eleven I was done. No emails to send, no reports to read or write, no plans to check. And I didn't know what to do with myself. I had all this time and no way to fill it. It was terrifying.

'So I went for a walk. I was heading towards Regent's Park, I think, planning to go to the zoo. It's what we did as kids for a treat. Raff was already gone. Maybe I was missing him. Anyway I ended up at Marylebone. There was a train to Hopeford and I liked the name—*hope*. So I jumped on.' She shook her head. 'It felt so daring, just travelling to a strange place on a whim. And then I got there and it was like another world.'

'It's very pretty.'

'And very quiet. I couldn't believe it. No shops were open, nobody was working, people were just walking, or gardening or cooking. When you live and work in London you forget that people live like that. We sell the tools, you know, the sheets and the candles and the saucepans and the garden furniture but it feels a little like make-believe. I didn't want it to be make-believe any more. I wanted it to be real.'

'So you moved?'

She laughed. 'No one could believe it; *I* didn't really believe it. It was the most impulsive thing I ever did. Well, until a few weeks ago anyway.'

'Are you happy there?'

There was a long pause. Nimbly she skirted a large group of tourists taking photos of a mime artist and the window shoppers milling outside the many boutiques.

'Yes,' she said finally. 'I am.'

'Not everything needs to be planned out,' he said softly. 'Sometimes just going with your instinct is the right path.'

She stopped and stared at him. 'Are we still talking about Hopeford?' she asked.

He shrugged. 'Just making conversation.'

'Well, don't.' She gestured at a glass door, sober and discreet in a Georgian building. 'We're here. Meet me afterwards? We still have to talk about work, remember?'

'I'll come in with you.' The words were out before he had a chance to think them through. 'There's always a lot of hanging around at these places. We can talk inside.'

Polly knew she should be attending to everything that Dr Vishal was saying but it was so alien she couldn't get a grip on it.

Was this really her body? Her future? Now the nausea was dying down she looked and felt the same as always. Maybe she had made a really embarrassing mistake and it had been a bug after all?

'You're fine, but I want you to make sure you do everything I am recommending.' The doctor broke into Polly's thoughts. 'Vitamins and rest and midwife appointments. Careful blood-pressure monitoring, some light exercise and proper food,' she said, frowning at Polly. 'You're too thin, Polly. If you can't or won't cook then there are some good meal-delivery services. Lots of protein and vegetables.'

'I'll arrange it,' Polly promised. It was almost a shame Gabe was moving out; he took food seriously enough.

'Are you ready?'

'For what?'

'To see your baby of course. If you go with Sasha she'll get you ready for your scan. We do them in house now although once your hospital referral goes through they'll want to scan again and sort out any extra blood tests.'

Polly followed Sasha, her brain whirling. A scan. Her hand fluttered to her stomach again. This was going to make the whole thing horribly real—unless it was a phantom-bug-baby after all.

Gabe was sitting on a chair in the corridor, his long legs sprawled out before him, frowning at the phone in his hand as he briskly typed out a message, but as Polly came close he shoved the phone into his pocket and got to his feet.

'Everything okay?'

'I think so. I have a long list of instructions. You'd like them; they use words like exercise and vitamins.'

'That's my language,' he agreed. 'Are you ready? We've still got an hour and a half until the meeting.'

'I've just…' Polly waved towards the nurse. 'A scan. To check everything is, you know, okay. I won't be long.'

'You're very welcome to come with us,' Sasha said with a bright smile. 'Ready to meet baby?'

Confused words of refusal rose to Polly's lips but when she started to speak nothing came out. Of course she didn't *need* company but it might be nice to have some backup, someone to reassure her that she wasn't imagining the whole thing.

Indecision was writ clearly on his face as he ran a hand over the dark stubble. 'Why not?' he said after a moment.

'No, don't worry,' she began but he was already on his feet.

'Come on,' he said. 'Let's go and see who's been causing you so much trouble.'

Gabe had seen more than his fair share of scan pictures. From the moment of his eldest niece's conception it felt as if he had been asked to admire thousands of fuzzy pictures of alien blobs. It wasn't just his family; more and more friends and colleagues were replacing their social media ID photos with what, he was fairly sure, was an identikit picture.

Secretly Gabe wondered if the whole thing was a scam, if there was just one photo that had been mocked up several years ago and was palmed off on every expectant couple. They probably made a fortune out of it.

The nurse led them into a small room. A chill shivered down Gabe's spine and his stomach clenched. The dull green walls, the blind at the window, the metal bed surrounded by machinery. It was a different country, a different patient and yet utterly, achingly familiar.

Old pains began to pulse in his limbs, scars to throb. He swallowed hard, trying to control his breathing. A cool hand touched his arm. Gabe braced himself for pity.

But all there was in the clear blue eyes was understanding. 'You can wait outside,' Polly said softly. 'It's fine.'

How did she know? How could she know?

He took a deep breath. 'I'm okay. Makes a nice change to not be the one on the bed.'

The hand lingered, squeezed. 'Thanks.' She didn't say anything else, just sat on the bed, her hands clasped, and waited for instructions.

Gabe folded himself into a chair while Polly was fussed over, the moment before frozen in his mind. He didn't often speak of his time in hospital, those days were over, but when it did come up there were usually two reactions: cloying pity or brisk heartiness.

It wasn't often anyone showed tact and understanding. He hadn't expected it from Polly; she was such a cat that walked alone. Why did she hide it? The sense of humour, the love of vintage accessories, her compassion? Did she feel that the human made her weak?

'Okay now, can you just lift your top?' The nurse's voice broke into his thoughts. The language was different but the tone exactly the same as the many, many nurses he had interacted with over the years: brisk, matter-of-fact.

Polly obediently rolled up the silk T-shirt, wincing as she did so, and Gabe tried not to laugh as he caught her expression—the carefully chosen top was going to get horribly creased. She was dressed for a board meeting not a doctor's appointment. Resolutely Gabe dragged his eyes away from the long legs lying supine on the bed, only to find himself staring at a flat stomach, the colour of warm honey.

It was a completely inappropriate time to stare but he couldn't help himself. She was on the thin side of slender, her ribs clearly visible. The cream fitted top set off the remains of her holiday tan; Gabe could hear her words echoing in his head: *'swimming naked in the sea'*. Just how much of her was honey brown?

He looked away quickly, trying to cleanse his mind of images of long limbs in clear waters, the hair floating languorously on the sea's surface. A lithe mermaid, dangerously desirable.

'This may be a little chilly,' the nurse warned her—*'it'll be utterly freezing'*, Gabe translated mentally and by Polly's quick shudder as the gel touched her belly knew he was right. 'Okay.' The nurse was smiling at him. 'Ready to say hello?'

The language was cloying, the situation somewhat surreal and the nurse evidently under the assumption that he was responsible for Polly's situation but any embarrassment dissolved the second the nurse ran the scanner over Polly's stomach. The screen wavered for a second and then there, in sharp focus, there it was.

Gabe stared at the screen. People used the word 'miracle' all the time until it lost any meaning but surely, *surely* this alien person floating around in Polly's body was a miracle?

He was so used to associating hospitals with pain and death he had completely forgotten what else they represented: life.

'It's still tiny,' the nurse told them. 'But perfect.'

Gabe looked over at Polly. Her head was turned to the screen; she was utterly transfixed. He didn't know if she had even heard the nurse.

'Is everything okay, as it should be?' he asked.

'It's still early days, you're what? Eleven weeks? But everything looks like it's right on track. The hospital will want to scan you again in about two to three weeks. All the details are in your pack. Do you want a photo?'

The ubiquitous photo. Suddenly Gabe could see the point of them after all. Why wouldn't you want to monitor every second?

He looked over at Polly but she didn't respond. But of course she would. Wouldn't she? '*Si*, I mean, please.'

Polly still hadn't spoken.

'Polly? Is everything okay?'

She blinked, once, twice as if released from a dream and then turned to him, her face transformed, lit up with an inner joy. It almost hurt to look at her.

'Oh yes,' she said. 'Everything is perfect.'

The contrast was completely surreal. One moment she was lying down, almost helpless as she deferred to the judgement and expertise of others, less than two hours later she had been on her feet, standing in front of a group of suited, booted, note-scribbling board members. Here she was the expert, the one in control, setting the pace and the agenda.

If she couldn't still feel the chill of the gel, sticky on her stomach, if she hadn't glanced down to see, with a shock of surprise, that she was no longer wearing the cream, fitted silk top but a sharply tailored pink shirt, she would think she had imagined her morning.

This was her future. A world of contrasts.

'That went well.' Her grandfather was sat at the head of the table. If his gaze lingered a little longingly on the bookcases that used to be filled with his belongings, if he eyed the pictures on the wall with barely hidden nostalgia then Polly couldn't blame him. The store was his life, his legacy.

As it was hers.

'Really interesting presentation, Pol,' Raff said. Her twin had spent his first meeting as a member of the Rafferty's board watching and listening intently but not jumping in. Not yet, although he had asked a few penetrating questions.

Polly knew him too well to think that he didn't have decided opinions—or that he wouldn't voice them—but he had been a supportive presence for her first official meeting as CEO.

She smiled at him, a rush of love for him flooding her. Despite their past disagreements and the long absences he was still part of her. And he would be part of her baby's life too, unconditionally, that went without saying. 'Thank you, Raff. For everything.'

'I love the pop-up idea—both in store and out. Where do you think you'll start?'

'In store,' she said, dragging her mind back to the matter at hand.

'We can use the centre of the Great Hall. It's mostly used for themed displays anyway. I've found this great designer who uses vintage fabrics and jewellery and reworks them into a more modern design but still with a hint of history. They're something really special and tie in brilliantly with the building and best of all she's completely unknown. We would be a great launch pad for her and it's exactly the kind of thing I'm looking for. Unique and creative.'

'And start branching out with the food when?' Her grandfather might sound casual but his gaze was as sharp as ever.

Much as she wanted to get started, Polly knew this couldn't be rushed. 'Next year. We've left it too late in the season to start properly—all the best festivals are booked up and there's no point starting anywhere else. But we are investigating doing a few surprise pop-ups locally so that we can test some concepts—Hyde Park, South Bank, Hampstead Heath. Picnics and Pimms, that kind of thing. We're in the process of applying for licences.'

'Dip your toe in, eh? Not a bad plan.' Her grandfather shifted his gaze over to Gabe, who was busy packing up his laptop. 'That's all very well, but I still don't know about this digital strategy of yours. It's risky.'

'Not mine, Gabe's,' Polly corrected. 'I agree, it is a lot of money—but you were the one who told me to hand all digital concerns over to him.'

'What's your gut instinct?'

She hesitated as Gabe snapped his briefcase shut and turned his attention to the trio at the table, his eyes intent on her. 'Truth is I'm torn,' she admitted. 'I think it's innovative and brilliant, but the technology is untried at this scale and the outlay huge. My heart tells me to go for it but my head is a lot more cautious. But, if we wait, and someone else gets in first, then we lose both the competitive edge and the PR advantage. Gabe, what do you think? Honestly.'

Gabe leant back against the wall, arms folded, and regarded them intently. Polly willed him to dig deep, to find something that convinced her, convinced her family.

'My parents use something a little similar,' he said after a long moment. 'It's not as all singing and dancing as the concept I presented but their web and digital presence is very different from their competitors'—much more interactive, presenting the vineyard, restaurant and B&B virtually just as it is in reality. Why don't you come over and see? See how the physical matches up with the online and Natalie can talk you through click-through rates, bookings and the uplift in spend.'

Polly shifted nervously. 'Go to Provence?' Go to Gabe's home. Meet his parents and sisters, see the place he had grown up in?

A further blurring of the lines she kept trying to draw—and ended up rubbing out.

'That's an excellent idea,' Raff said warmly. 'I think that's exactly what we need, to see something similar and grasp just how it works in practice. You should go, Polly.' He looked at Gabe. 'If Pol agrees it's a goer then you have my vote.'

'I agree.' Her grandfather was looking at her thoughtfully. 'Take your time, look at every angle and then report back. If Raff and I are a yes then the rest will fall into line. But it needs your un-equivocal approval, Polly. It's too much of a gam-ble for half-hearted efforts.'

'If we go this weekend the wine festival is on.' Gabe was checking his phone as he spoke. 'They have all kinds of stalls—wine, obviously, food, entertainment. Could be good research for planning just what the Rafferty pop-up brand will be.'

Polly nodded, to all intents and purposes solely focused on the matter at hand—but her mind was churning. This was all a little cosy.

She had spent the last week trying to re-estab-lish much-needed boundaries—and so evidently had he. Now they had separate offices, now he spent so little time in Hopeford, she could con-vince herself that her evening of weakness was a one-off anomaly. A symptom of shock.

But if that *was* the case then what harm could a weekend do? It was just a working weekend like any other, she reminded herself. In fact it was probably a good thing, a chance to prove to herself that she was in control, in every way. 'It sounds perfect,' she said. 'Count me in.'

CHAPTER SEVEN

'WHAT A SHAME we didn't get to see some of Paris, but it was easier to fly in to Toulouse. I would have liked to have shown you around Desmoulins.' British retail royalty meeting the cream of Parisian style; it would have been an interesting introduction.

Now they were in his country, on his turf, Gabe was back behind the wheel, waving a protesting Polly into the passenger seat, refusing to listen to her attempts to direct him; no phone sat nav could possibly know the roads, the shortcuts better than the returning native.

'I've never been to Paris.' She was looking out of the window, seemingly absorbed in the scenery. It was worth looking at, the undulating hills and bright fields of lavender and sunflowers. At one point Provence had felt too rural, too stiflingly parochial to hold him. Now his blood thrilled to the scented air. He was home.

'You must have. A woman like you! Business, romance, shopping…'

She was shaking her head. 'Nope. Business I conduct in London. Romance?' She smiled wryly. 'I didn't really take time in my twenties for romantic breaks and the least said about this year, the better.' She rubbed her stomach. Gabe had noticed how often her hand crept there instinctively, unthinkingly, as if she had a primal need to connect with the life within.

'And I shop at Rafferty's of course. Or Milan or New York if I do want a busman's holiday.'

'But…' He was incredulous. Surely everyone came to Paris at some point in their lives. 'But what about fashion week?'

She shook her head. 'That's the buyers' job. I can't predict the next season's hits and I don't need to. I pay people with far more flair to do it.'

Oh, she had flair. It helped that she was almost model tall and model thin; it made it easy for her to wear clothes designed with willowy slenderness in mind. But she wore them with a panache that didn't come from the designer. It was innate. Even today, casual in a pair of skinny jeans and a yellow flowery top, she turned heads.

'But why? It takes what? Two and a half hours by train? It's a day trip.'

Polly smiled. A little self-consciously. 'It's silly.'

Gabe turned to look at her. Now he was intrigued; what on earth made Polly Rafferty blush in embarrassment?

'I can keep a secret.'

'I know.' She winced. 'You already know far too many of mine. I can't give you any more.'

She had a point. It was odd, knowing things not even her brother knew. Tied them together in a way that wasn't as unwelcome as it should be. He should even the score, make them equals.

Gabe turned his concentration back to the road ahead, navigating a tight bend before answering. 'That's fair. How about I tell you two of mine and then you answer?'

She leant back in her seat and considered. 'They have to be embarrassing secrets. Or deeply personal. Things you have never told anyone.'

'Okay.' He took a deep breath. Gabe was a businessman; he had always done what he needed to to get ahead. A little stretching of the truth here, aking a gamble on an assumption there. Nothing shonest or illegal—more a prevarication.

But he couldn't prevaricate here; Polly was right. He did owe her a secret or two.

He just had so many to choose from. It might be nice to let one or two of them out, to lighten the load.

Gabe concentrated on the road ahead, his hands gripping the steering wheel so tightly his knuckles were white. 'When I was ill I hated my parents so much I couldn't even look at them when they came to visit.'

He heard her inhale, a long, shuddering breath. But she didn't protest or tell him he must be mistaken. 'Why?'

'Because they hurt so damn much. Every needle in my vein pierced them twice as hard, when I retched, they doubled over. My illness nearly killed them. They wanted me to live, to fight, so badly that when I slipped back I knew I was failing them. My illness failed them.'

He could feel it again: the shame of causing so much hurt, the anger that they needed him to be strong when it was almost too much. The responsibility of having to fight, to stay alive for them.

'They must love you a lot.' Her voice was a little wistful.

'They do. And I love them but it's a lot. You have to be strong for yourself in that situation, single-minded. Their need distracted me. Added too much pressure.'

'Is that why you don't want children?'

He thought back to her scan, to the life pulsing inside her, the unexpected protectiveness that had engulfed him and picked his words carefully.

'Our lives are so fragile, our happiness so dependent on others. I've been cancer free for nearly ten years, Polly. But it could come back. I don't want to put a wife or a child through the suffering I put my parents through. I don't want to suffer like that for someone else. Is it worth it?'

There was a pause and he knew without looking that her hand would be back at her midriff.

'I hope so,' she said after a while.

He continued driving while she busied herself with her phone. 'You still haven't told me your second secret.' She was looking away again. It was like being in the seal of the confessional: intimate and confidential.

Gabe didn't even consider before he answered. 'Ever since I kissed you in the office I've wanted ɔ do it again.'

Another silence. This one more loaded. He was achingly aware of her proximity, of her bare arms, the blonde hair piled precariously in a loose knot, the hitch in her breath as he spoke.

His words had unlocked a desire he didn't even know he carried, one he had hidden, locked down. The kiss had been totally inappropriate. They were colleagues; she was his boss. He didn't want or need anything complicated—and nothing about Polly Rafferty was simple.

She was prickly and bossy. She didn't know the names of half her staff and was rude to and demanding of the ones she did know. She worked all the time. She was pregnant.

Sure, she was conventionally pretty with her mass of blonde silky hair, her dark blue eyes and legs that went on for ever but that was just the surface. It was the inappropriately intimate conversations with cars, that carefully hidden vulnerability and her way of looking into a man's soul and seeing just what it was that made him tick that made her dangerous.

It made her formidable. It made her utterly desirable.

'What does the tree mean?' Her words pierced

the thickened atmosphere, the soft voice a little unsteady, her hands twisting on her lap.

'*Pardon?*'

'Your tattoo? What does it mean?'

His mouth twisted. 'My mother didn't cry once during any of my treatment but she wept when I showed her that tattoo. And not with pride.'

'I think it's beautiful.' Her voice was almost shy.

'It's life,' he told her. 'I wanted my body to reflect growth and hope, not death.'

'My mother told me you should visit Paris to fall in love.' Polly changed the subject abruptly. 'That's why I've never been.'

'You've never fallen in love?'

'I've been in "like",' she said. 'I've been in companionable comfort. I've desired.' Did her eyes flicker towards Gabe at the last word?

His chest tightened at the thought, the blood pulsing hot and thick around his body.

'But, no. I haven't been in love.' She bit her lip. 'That is rather shameful for a woman of thirty-one, isn't it?'

'*Non.*' The word was strong, vehement. 'Real love is rare, precious. Many of us will never experience it.' He'd thought he'd found it once. Had watched it slip away.

'My mother left home when I was eight. Our father died a couple of years later but he was in a home all that time.' Her voice faltered. 'We found him, Raff and I. He'd had a stroke. He needed full-time care and we were a mess. My mother just couldn't cope. People always took care of her, you see. She was one of those fragile women, all eyes and a way of looking at you as if you were all that mattered. She went away for a rest and just never returned, found someone else to take care of her.'

'I'm sorry.' The words were inadequate.

'Oh, it was a long time ago, and I think I always knew. Knew she couldn't be relied on. It was harder on Raff. He absolutely adored her. But for some reason I never forgot her words. She said she'd been to Paris before, with friends, boyfriends, but when she went with Daddy the city turned into a magical wonderland and she knew...'

'Knew what?'

'That she was in love,' she said simply. 'And she made me promise her, promise I would never go to Paris until I was sure I was ready to fall in love.

It's funny, I have spent my whole life not being my mother, not relying on anyone else, always doing my duty. But I kept my promise.'

Her mouth curved into a reminiscent smile. 'She also told me to always wear lipstick, make sure my hair was brushed and to wear the best shoes I can afford. I never forgot that advice either.'

'Even on the Inca trail?'

She exhaled, an amused bubble of laughter. 'Especially then.'

'I hope you get to Paris one day.' She deserved it, deserved to have the trip of her dreams, to experience the world's most romantic city with somebody who loved her by her side.

But the thought of her strolling hand in hand through the city streets with some unknown other, cruising down the Seine, kissing on the Pont des Arts, made his whole body tense up, jealousy coursing through his veins.

It was ridiculous; he had no reason to be jealous.

Jealousy implied need. Implied caring. Sure he liked Polly, respected her, was attracted to her. But that was all.

If she worked somewhere else, if she weren't pregnant then she would be perfect—for a while.

She was as busy as he was, as focused as he was, she wouldn't want him to take care of her, to text or call five times a day. She wouldn't care if he went away for a weekend's training or decided to pull an all-nighter at the office.

And when she talked about the likes, the companionable comforts and the desires of her past there was no hint of regret. She moved on without a second's thought. Just as he did.

But she *was* his boss and she *was* going to have a baby and there was no point dwelling on what-might-have-beens. Because the boss situation would change one day but the baby situation most definitely wouldn't. And that made her even more off-limits than ever. She deserved someone who would want a family, someone to take her to Paris.

'You may even fall in love there,' he added.

'Maybe.' She didn't sound convinced. 'It's a fairytale, though, isn't it? Not real life. Because, although Mummy had that perfect moment, it didn't mean enough in the end, didn't stop her bailing when things became rough.'

'No.' There was nothing else to say.

She took out a few pins and let her hair fall, before gathering it up and twisting it into a tighter knot, a few strands escaping in the breeze. 'It was a sharp lesson. If you rely on someone else you are vulnerable. You need to be self-sufficient, to protect yourself.' She sighed. 'It would be nice to meet someone who understood that, who didn't think being independent means not caring.'

She shook her head. 'One day I'll go to Paris, on my own. Or take the baby.'

'You could go to Disneyland.'

She grimaced. 'I am so not ready for this.'

Gabe glanced over. 'You will be,' he said. 'I think you are going to do just fine.'

There was something intimidating about meeting other people's families. Mingling, small talk, conferences, cocktail parties, those posed no fear at all for Polly. But the intimacy and warmth of family homes chilled her.

Even at school she'd hated the invites back to other girls' houses for the holidays. It was all so alien: in-jokes and traditions, bickering, knowing your place was secure. So different from the formality of her grandparents' house, a place more like a museum than a home for two children.

Throw in a different language, a tangle of small

children and in-laws and her arrival at the Beau-fils chateau was a scene right out of her worst fears. She was seized upon, hugged, kissed and exclaimed over by what felt like an endless stream of people.

'It is lovely to meet you.' Madame Beaufils linked an arm through Polly's and whisked her through the imposing front door.

'Thank you so much for having me.' Polly did her best to relax. She wasn't really that comfort-able with physicality, more of a handshake than a hug person, but she couldn't work out how to dis-entangle herself without causing offence. 'Your home is beautiful.'

No fakery needed here. Polly had grown up ac-customed to a luxurious home; her grandfather still lived in the old Queen Anne manor house in the Berkshire countryside that she and Raff had been brought up in. But the weathered old cha-teau with its ivy-covered walls, surrounded by lovingly tended gardens that stretched into the vineyards beyond, had something her childhood home lacked.

It had heart.

There were pictures everywhere: photos, framed

children's paintings, portraits and certificates. The furniture in the huge hall at the centre of the house was well chosen, chic but loved, the sofa a little frayed, the mirror spotted with age.

'It's a mess,' Gabe's mother said dismissively. 'We put our money into renovating the old barns for the B&B and wedding business, and for turning the wings of the house into apartments for Natalie and Claire and their families. But I like it like this. It feels as if my children are still here with me.' She looked longingly at a large photo of a laughing, dark-eyed girl.'

'That's Celine,' she said with a sigh. 'My biggest fear is that she will meet someone in New Zealand and never return to us. It was worse when Gabe was in the States. Paris was better but at least he's just over the Channel. I can almost breathe again.'

It must be claustrophobic to be needed like that, Polly thought with a stab of sympathy for the absent Celine. But a small, irrepressible part of her couldn't help wondering what it would be like. Her grandmother was certainly miffed if Polly didn't meet her for tea and accompany her shopping when she was in town, and her grandfather liked updates on the store. But neither of them needed Polly for herself. Any granddaughter would have done.

'I've put you in the blue room.' Madame Beaufils led Polly up the grand circular staircase dominating the great hall. 'It has its own en-suite so you will be quite private. Why don't you take a moment to freshen up and then come back down for some lunch before we show you around?' She smiled. 'Natalie is very excited at the thought of showing off her website to you. She has been compiling numbers all week!'

The room she showed Polly to was lovely. It was very simple with high ceilings, dark polished floorboards and whitewashed walls with a huge wooden bedstead dominating one end of the room. The bed was made up with a blue throw and pillows; it looked so inviting Polly didn't dare sit down in case the fatigue pulsing away at her temples took over.

Instead she walked over to the large French windows and flung open the shutters to step out onto the narrow balcony. Her room was at the back of the house overlooking the peaceful-looking garden and the rows of vines beyond. She had never seen anything so vibrant, even on her travels—

the green of the vines contrasting with the purple hues of the lavender in the distance, set off by an impossibly blue sky. Polly breathed in, feeling the rich air fill her lungs and, for the first time since that devastating conversation with her grandfather all those months ago, she felt at peace.

She reluctantly tore herself away from the view and took her toiletry bag into the pretty bathroom adjoining her room, emptying out her compact and lipgloss. It was time to apply her armour.

Or was it?

Polly stared at the deep berry red she favoured and then slowly set it back down.

She didn't need to hide. Not today. Instead she loosened her hair and brushed it out, allowing it to fall naturally down her back.

With one last longing glance at the inviting-looking bed, Polly took a deep breath and opened the door. She was ready.

She found the family in the garden, congregated around a large cast-iron table set under a large shady tree. It was already set for lunch and at the sight of the plates piled high with breads, salad, cheese and meat Polly's increasingly capricious appetite perked up.

Oh no, what if it was one of those days? It was all or nothing at the moment; mostly nothing, but when she did want to eat she had no stop mechanism. She hoped she didn't eat the Beaufils family out of house and home.

She could imagine them, gathered together in twenty years' time, telling tales of the Englishwoman who couldn't stop eating.

Polly leant on the corner of the house content just to watch them for a moment. Everyone was talking, words tumbling out, interrupting each other with expansive hand gestures. Polly's French was pretty good but she was completely confused by the rapid crossfire of laughing conversation.

The laughter was loud and often. Each peal rang through her, making it harder and harder to take a step forward, to interrupt. Not wanting to break into the reunion, for the lively chatter to turn into the inevitable formal chitchat a stranger's presence would cause.

And the longer she stood there, the more impossible that step seemed.

She had never seen Gabe so utterly relaxed. Sitting at the head of the table, he had one plump toddler held firmly on his knee, another was crawling at his feet, attempting occasionally to climb up his denim-clad legs. His mother was pouring him wine, one sister showing him something on her iPad, his father grasping his arm as he made his point.

He was totally immersed, somehow paying attention to each member of his family. A smile of thanks, a nod of acknowledgement, a firm capturing of sticky fingers. Son, brother, uncle, the heart of his family. How could he want to escape this? If this was Polly's family she would never ever want to leave.

It was as if he could hear her thoughts. Gabe's head snapped up and he looked straight over at Polly, his dark gaze unwavering. She didn't want him to think her a coward, wanted to step out with her head held high but she was paralysed, held still by the understanding in his eyes.

She should have felt exposed, weak, but instead it was as if he was cloaking her in warmth, sending strength into suddenly aching limbs. It was almost painful when he dragged his eyes away, handing the toddler on his knee to his mother and scooping up the one by his feet as he rose gracefully out of his chair, walking over to Polly and expertly avoiding the small hands trying to grab his nose.

'*Bonjour*, Polly, this is Mathilde. She doesn't speak English yet but you must forgive her. Her French is terrible too.'

'Your French was terrible too when you were two, and it's not much better now,' interrupted a petite dark-haired woman with a vivacious grin as she came over to join them. She lifted the protesting small girl out of her uncle's arms, cuddling her close with a consoling kiss before turning to Polly.

'We must all be a bit much for you. It gets very loud when we are en masse. Especially when we have all the babies with us. I'm Natalie. I'm sure you didn't get a chance to work out who was who earlier.'

'It's lovely to meet you.' Polly couldn't help her gaze dropping to focus on the woman's large bump.

Natalie followed her gaze and grimaced. 'I know, I am enormous.' She shook her head ruefully. 'The doctor assures me it's not twins. I blame Maman's cooking. There's nothing like eating for two.'

'Not at all,' Polly said quickly. 'I was just thinking how well you look.'

Well. Happy and secure. Could that be her future?

'Come, sit and eat. Would you like some wine? *Non?* How about some grape juice made from our own vines? It's very refreshing.'

Polly allowed herself to be led to the table, to have her glass filled with the chilled juice, her plate filled with a tempting selection of breads, salads and meats, and did her best to join in with the conversation, which kept lapsing into French.

'En anglais,' Madame Beaufils said reprovingly. She turned to Polly. 'I am so sorry, Polly. You must think us very rude.'

'Not at all. I think you are very happy to see Gabe. Please, don't speak English on my account. It will do me good to try and get along. My French is sadly rusty.'

'But so many of our hotel guests are English it does us good to speak it,' Claire said. Gabe's oldest sister was the quietest of the family, much of her time taken in attending to one of the two small children sitting by her side. A third slept quietly in a pram under the tree. 'I want these three to grow up with perfect English.'

Polly eyed the eldest child; he was no more than three, she thought, although children's ages were a mystery to her. One she would soon be solving. Despite many longing glances at a football in the middle of the lawn he was sitting upright on his chair eating daintily. 'He's very good,' she said. Maybe French children *did* have better manners.

Claire grinned. 'He's been bribed. Uncle Gabe will come and play trains with him if he eats all his lunch and behaves. Don't let him fool you. He's not usually this angelic.'

'How do you do it?' Polly looked from Claire to Natalie, both so laid-back, dressed simply but elegantly, not a hair out of place. 'Raise them and run this place?'

'With help!' Claire said emphatically and Natalie nodded in laughing agreement.

'I have an au pair, Maman is always on hand and my husband does a great deal.'

Polly smiled automatically but her mind was racing, calculating. She didn't have a mother or a husband—but she could buy in help. After all, she paid people to clean her house, buy her groceries, mow her lawn. Why not to raise her child?

Polly put the bread she was holding back on her plate untasted. It sounded so cold. She looked over at the small boy trying so hard to be good and wished he were free to run free, to tear into his food with gusto. That her presence didn't constrain him.

She didn't want to recreate her childhood, to raise a perfectly behaved child painfully trying to live up to impossibly high expectations. She wanted…she wanted *this*. Loud, argumentative, affectionate and close. If she was going to have a child then she wanted a real family: wellies and mud and a big golden dog, the whole lot.

Well, maybe not a dog; Mr Simpkins would never cope.

Summoning up her best French, she leant over to the small boy. 'Bonjour, Jean. I love trains,' she said. 'When you've finished eating do you think you could show me?'

Jean put his bread down and regarded her with

solemn dark eyes. 'I have cars too,' he said after a pause. 'Do you like cars too?'

'I adore cars,' Polly told him. 'Especially old ones.'

CHAPTER EIGHT

'YOUR FAMILY ARE lovely.'

It seemed odd to be alone with Gabe again after twenty-four hours of almost continuous company. After playing cars with Jean for a surprisingly enjoyable hour she had had a comprehensive tour of the vineyard and B&B accommodation followed by another long, laughter-filled family meal, this one enhanced by Claire and Natalie's charming husbands.

Visiting a vineyard and refusing to sample any of the products might seem eccentric but nobody had commented. Thank goodness she was past the sickness stage, otherwise she might have disgraced herself as soon as she entered the bottling room and storage cellars with their strong, distinct, alcoholic odour.

Gabe slid her a sidelong look. 'They like you.'

A glow spread through her at his words. She had been at the vineyard for such a short time, a stranger speaking a different language, but she felt a connection to the Beaufils family. It was nice to know it wasn't one-sided.

'Especially Jean,' he added. 'I think you've ousted me from number one. Luckily for me Mathilde still thinks I'm perfect.'

Polly rolled her eyes. 'They all seem very blinkered where you're concerned. Did I see your mother make your smoothie this morning?'

'She likes to,' he said with an annoying smirk, every inch the youngest child. 'I even managed to drag Papa out for a run. Well, more of a jog but it was a start. He eats too much—drinks too much. It's an occupational hazard.'

'How does your father feel about Claire and Natalie's innovations?' Polly asked. There were no traces of the power struggles she had experienced with her grandfather—but they could be good at putting on a public face. She knew all about that; public solidarity was part of the Rafferty code.

'He is overjoyed they are still at home, that they love the vineyard as much as he does.' Gabe pulled an expressive face. 'If he could keep us all there he would. I know he hopes Celine will come back and take over the wine production.'

'And you?'

'There's no place for me there, not now. My horizons are wider. I return home for holidays, weekends. I don't have the time to come back often.'

'I don't think there's any lack of ambition at the vineyard.' Polly had spent the morning with Natalie looking at all the digital innovations the Frenchwoman had introduced. It was impressive, a seamless interface between the physical world and the digital marketplace. 'Natalie is far ahead of much bigger businesses. There's an app for everything. And I think Claire plans to make it *the* premier events and hospitality venue in the country. She'll do it too, if she has the capital.'

'I can help out there.'

'I think they'd rather have your input than your money. Oh, I don't mean come back home to live. But they miss you.' She grinned at him. 'Talk about the prodigal son. If you get this kind of reaction after a few weeks in London I can't imagine what your mother feeds Celine when she comes home.'

'A full fatted calf.' He looked over at her. 'What did they say?'

A flush rose on her cheeks. She didn't want Gabe to think she'd been talking about him, probing for secrets and tales. But his family had been all too eager to share stories with her.

Almost as if she were his girlfriend, not his boss.

A wave of longing swept through her as unexpected as it was unwelcome. What would it be like to be welcomed into the bosom of a family such as this? To be part of a large, loving, chaotic throng? To have a place around the enormous scrubbed pine table that dominated the kitchen? To know your steps in the carefully choreographed dance of a family meal. Even Mathilde and Jean had gone straight to a drawer to collect and fold napkins. The sons-in-law were kept busy fetching and carrying.

Polly alone had had no role. The guest, set apart.

'They said you don't come home enough but they understand that you're busy.' Polly chose her words carefully. 'That as they look at expanding it would be good to have your input, only they know how it's hard for you to get away.'

Their eyes followed him everywhere, their need echoing out. They adored him, would absorb him back in if he gave them the chance. Polly could see how it smothered him, why he stayed away even as she wondered what it would be like, to be loved so comprehensively.

'Papa often talks about expanding.' Gabe was dismissive. 'Yet, he never does.'

'He might do if you were there to talk it through with him.' Polly could hear the tart note in her voice but didn't try to rein it in. 'Your sisters are specialists, great at what they do but very focused. You however are trained in managing the bigger picture. You should give him some time beyond a morning jog.'

There was a pained silence. 'One day here and you're the expert on my family.'

Words of apology rose to her lips but she swallowed them back. 'I don't need to be an expert. It's completely plain to anyone with eyes. I'm not saying move back home, but you could talk his plans through with him, advise him.'

'Maybe.'

'I know you needed to get away—and you did, you created a life away from them. Well...' she considered him '...you created a *career* away from them.'

Gabe's mouth was set tight, a muscle pulsing in his jaw. 'I don't see the distinction.'

'I know,' she said sadly. 'You and I are birds of a feather. We think success at work, achieving career goals is all that matters, all that defines us. But, Gabe, I *had* nothing else. The only approval I ever got was work-related—and I begrudged it. But you? You could announce you were giving it all up tomorrow to go back and, I don't know, create art out of vine leaves and they would still welcome you home and support you all the way.'

His mouth twitched. 'Art out of vine leaves?'

'It might be a thing.'

He didn't say anything for a few minutes, his eyes set on the road ahead. Polly sat back in her seat, losing herself in the vibrant scenery. What must it be like to grow up surrounded by so much colourful beauty?

'Why does it matter to you?' His words were so unexpected it took a moment for Polly to comprehend them.

'Why does what matter?' But she knew what he meant.

'My family, my place there.'

Her cheeks heated. 'It doesn't mean a thing to

me personally,' she said. 'But I like your parents, your sisters. It seems a shame, that's all. I like you...' Her words hung there. Polly wanted to grab them, take them back.

But they *were* out there. So she might as well be completely honest. 'I like you,' she said again. *In for a penny,* she thought.

'I'm not keen on the workaholic who flirts with my assistant, the smell of those smoothies would turn my stomach even if I wasn't pregnant and I have very strong, negative views on people who turn up to work in Lycra cycling shorts.' Even if they did look as good as on Gabe. You had to have good legs to pull off the tightly fitting shorts. Gabe rocked them.

Some staff members had taken to standing near the staff entrance when he came back from his lunch time bike ride.

'Don't spare my feelings.' But there was a quirk at the side of his mouth as he tried to hide a reluctant smile.

'I really dislike the way you take one girl out for a drink and another the next day. I know you don't cross any lines or break promises, but it creates discord and I won't have that in my store. But...'

she took a deep breath '…I do admire the way you remember everyone's name and what they do. I am a little envious of the rapport you have with my staff already. I don't doubt you'll be a CEO by thirty because you're focused and innovative and put the hours in.'

'Should I be blushing?'

'And I don't know what I would have done without you last week.' There, she had said it.

'Oh, Polly.' He shook his head, the smile gone. 'You would have been absolutely fine.'

'Maybe,' she agreed. 'I am used to doing things alone. I would have *coped*. I'd have had to. But it was nice not having to. Maybe it's the time I had away, maybe it's the hormones whooshing around turning everything upside down, but I am actually glad, glad that there is going to be something in my life apart from work. It may not be planned, the circumstances aren't ideal but I think the baby is a good thing for me.'

She smiled ruefully. 'Of course if you repeat that to anyone I will kill you.'

'I'd expect nothing less.'

'But you already have things outside work. Nieces and nephews and a family—and you keep yourself apart. I know why, I understand why. I just wonder…' She paused, trying to pick her words carefully. 'I just think maybe it's time you open yourself back up to them. Don't you think you've punished them enough?'

'I'm not punishing them.'

'Aren't you?' She pulled at her hair, twisting it round in her hand as she looked at him, at the set of his jaw, the line of his mouth. The dark chill in his eyes. 'Punishment? Atonement? Proving something? Whatever it is you're doing it's been ten years. I think it's time you gave them a break. I think you should give yourself a break. Before it's too late.'

Polly's words echoed round and round in Gabe's head despite his attempts to push them away, far away out of his subconscious.

Punishment.

She was right, damn her. But not as right as she thought she was. He wasn't punishing them.

He was punishing himself. For falling ill, for causing them such pain and anxiety.

For all the petty, nasty resentment he had allowed to build up during that long year of pain.

Resentment towards his parents for their need and worry. Towards his sisters for their health.

He didn't speak for the rest of the journey. Polly didn't try to engage him in conversation, scribbling notes in her ever-present notebook instead but occasionally shooting him concerned glances.

Glances he pretended not to see. If he didn't engage then he didn't need to speak and he could lock it all back up, deep inside.

Where it needed to be.

It took a while to find a parking space in the small riverside town of Vignonel. Sleepy for fifty weeks of the year, it was transformed into an international hub by the annual food and drink festival held there every summer. Over the years it had grown to include culture, local crafts and music, and every year thousands of people descended there from all over the world to dance, drink and eat.

They had all descended today, it seemed.

'This is where we've been going wrong,' Polly said after they were finally parked and had begun to thread their way through the main thoroughfare that led towards the main town square. 'We don't go out and find our suppliers any more.

People come and pitch to us. Chris and the rest of his team should be here, searching out the best local producers and stocking them.'

'Yes.' But he barely heard her words, his attention snagged by the large church dominating the town square. His heart began to speed up and despite the heat of the day a cold sweat covered his hands.

He swallowed, a bitter taste coating his mouth. 'There's a lot to see,' he managed to say in as normal a tone as possible. 'We'll cover more ground if we split up.'

A fleeting expression flashed in Polly's blue eyes. For a moment Gabe wondered if he had hurt her feelings but dismissed the arrogant notion as her head snapped up and she became her usual focused self.

'Good idea.' She pulled out her notebook and pen. 'We'll compare notes when we meet up. Look out for suppliers but I am more interested in what makes a stall successful, what draws people in. The look, the branding, the offer.'

'The technology?' Gabe couldn't help giving the leather-bound book a pointed look and Polly hugged it to her chest protectively.

'What? I don't have to worry about the battery running out or a system relapse wiping everything.'

'No, you just have to keep it dry and hope you don't lose it.' They had reached an information point and he picked up a map and guide, handing it to Polly. Her hand was cool, soft. Comforting. A sudden urge to take it in his, to stroll through the streets together, no notebooks, no reports, no memories, hit him but he pushed it aside. It took more effort than he cared for to refocus.

'I promised Claire I'd call in at her tourism and marketing pavilion.' Was she really so oblivious to his momentary inner struggle? Evidently so. She was frowning at the map in utter concentration. 'If I look at that part of the market why don't you go into the wine quarter to start? Your father's there on the regional wine stand this afternoon. And no...' her eyes met his clearly '...I'm not interfering, just being polite.'

She held his gaze, cool and self-possessed before inclining her head, a curiously old-fashioned gesture. 'I'll see you back here, then.'

Gabe watched as she swivelled and walked away, her head held high, the dark gold sweep of hair still loose, covering the slim line of her back. It was odd to see her hair down, not in the customary loose knot, for her to leave it unfettered. It made her seem younger, relaxed.

What would it be like to tangle his hand in that hair? Let the silken tresses fold around his fingers?

She was wearing the pink dress she'd bought at the vintage fair and as Gabe followed the proud, straight figure as she disappeared into the crowd he had a curious sense of being out of time.

Okay, time to push such fanciful thoughts out of his head, time to get on. To find his father, say hello, compliment him on the stall and the vintage just as Polly suggested.

As for the rest? It was ridiculous. He wasn't punishing them. He was protecting them.

Protecting himself.

If you had no ties then you couldn't get hurt. It was that simple.

The food and drink quarter was situated on one of the several windy streets that led off the square, opposite the church. Just a few minutes' walk up there and he would be among old friends and neighbours, watching his father do what he did best—enthusing about wine.

A smile curved his lips as he pictured the scene: a laughing group of tourists pulled in by his father's practised patter, sipping and tasting before parting with what would no doubt be a considerable amount of money.

Just a few minutes' walk. He should go, say hi.

He could even offer to help.

Gabe stood for a moment and then slowly turned to face the church.

A deep breath shuddered through him as if an icy fist had clenched his heart.

He hadn't set foot in that church for ten years and yet he could clearly picture the aged, wooden beams, see the sunlight dancing through the coloured glass in the ancient windows, the expression on the faces of the cold marble statues. He could smell the incense as it burned hot and heavy.

He could see the coffin.

Without conscious thought, without decision, he walked across the tree-lined square, away from the festival, past the church, to the narrow street that led out of town. Towards the old walled cemetery.

To Marie's grave.

Was it really ten years since he had stood by the open grave, pale faced and dry eyed as the white coffin had been slowly and solemnly lowered in?

White! She would have been horrified! Demanded black and velvet with silver clasps—or nothing at all, a quiet spot in a wooded glade. No X to mark the spot.

But burials weren't for the dead, they were for those left behind and her parents had needed every last trimming to get them through the day.

His mouth tightened. He hadn't written or contacted the Declors for years, unable to face another visit down memory lane. Not wanting to sit in the claustrophobic *salon*, sipping wine while looking through photo albums preserving the memory of a dead girl, pink cheeked and full of health. He had never known that girl. The Marie he had known had been like him, clad with a hospital pallor.

They were supposed to live or die together. He hadn't kept his part of the deal. Had she known, when she slipped away, that he wouldn't be joining her? Not yet.

Which was the worst betrayal? That he hadn't died with her or that she hadn't lived with him?

Had she forgiven him? He wasn't sure he had forgiven her yet. Or himself.

'Gabe?'

He jumped, a shiver running down his spine at the softly breathed words.

'Gabe!' No, not a ghost. Not unless Marie had developed a clipped English accent in the last ten years, had swapped the Converse low tops for high-heeled sandals that tapped smartly on the old cobbles.

He stopped and turned. Waited. Relieved to have the present intrude on the past.

'Claire was so busy I didn't like to disturb her.' Polly stopped as she reached the tall figure, her hand automatically going up to nervously knot her hair, only to fall away as she spoke. 'I wondered if maybe you wanted some lunch, if I could buy you some lunch. I…er…I crossed a line earlier. I need to apologise.'

She let a shuddering breath go and waited.

Lunch, work, an excuse not to face up to the past, to push it away for another decade.

'That would be nice,' he said after a long moment. 'But there's somewhere I need to go first. Polly, I'd really like it if you came with me.'

The river rushed along, white-topped as it bubbled over rocks and dropped over mini falls. The path along it was flat, easy walking. Left the mind free to wander.

Polly wasn't entirely sure that this was a good thing. She searched for something to say.

Nothing.

Now didn't seem appropriate to discuss work and she had already ventured into personal territory once that day. Look how well that had gone down, a clear indication to mind her own business.

Only… It was just…

He had asked her to come along.

She hadn't gone all the way into the rather macabre cemetery with its carved headstones, statues and family vaults, as different from a tidy Church Of England graveyard as a Brie from Cheddar, rather she had waited by the wall as Gabe had walked steadily to a white marble gravestone, topped with a carved cherub, and dropped to one knee in front of it. He had stayed there for five minutes, head bowed. Polly couldn't tell if he was weeping, praying or just frozen in silent contemplation. Either way discomforting shivers had rippled down her spine.

She had witnessed something deeply personal.

So she should say something, right? Wasn't that the normal thing to do when someone allowed you to see a part of their soul?

Only it had never happened before. She had no compass for this kind of thing. No guidance.

Even at her very proper boarding school there hadn't been a lesson on how to handle this kind of situation.

How to greet an ambassador? Yes. Royal garden party etiquette? Of course.

But this? She was clueless. She was going to have to go in blind.

'Are you okay?'

Not the most insightful or original icebreaker in the world, but it was a start.

'Oui.' Gabe turned, looked at her, the dark eyes unreadable. 'Thank you.'

Polly stopped, tilting her head up to meet his gaze. 'What for? I didn't do anything.'

He shrugged. 'For being there. I needed a friend.'

Her eyes dropped; she was suddenly, oddly shy. 'I owe you.' Unable to resume looking at him, she started walking again and he fell into step beside her. 'Who was it?'

He sighed, low and deep. 'Who was your first love, Polly?'

'My what?' Flustered, she pushed her hair away from her face. 'I don't know. I thought we'd already covered that I don't really do love.'

'But there must have been someone, a crush, a passion. Someone who made your world that bit more exciting, your pulse beat that bit faster. Someone who made your blood heat up with just the thought of them.' His voice was low, his accent more pronounced than usual; each word hit her deep inside, burning.

You.

But she didn't say the word; she couldn't. That wasn't who she was, what they were. They might have crossed a line from colleagues to friends but the next line, from friends to lovers, was too far, too high, too unattainable.

And Polly didn't have many friends. She didn't want to screw this new understanding up.

First love? She dragged her mind back, to her lonely teenage years.

'I had a huge crush on my school friend's brother,' she admitted. 'I was sixteen and staying there one Christmas holidays. He kissed me on New Year and I went back to school convinced we were an item. When I next saw him he was with his girlfriend and barely acknowledged me.' She grimaced. 'I wept for a week. What a silly idiot I was.'

'*Non.*' To her surprise he reached over and took her hand. His long fingers laced through hers. Every millimetre where his skin touched hers was immediately sensitised, tiny electric shocks darting up her arm, piercing the core of her.

She shivered, all her attention on her hand, on her fingers, on the way he was touching her, the light caress.

It wasn't enough.

Just friends, remember? she told herself sternly. But who was she fooling? As *if* it were enough.

'That's how we learn, that complete single-mindedness of the teenage heart.'

'Learn what?'

His fingers tightened on hers. 'That feelings are not always worth the price.'

'Gabe.' Her voice was husky with the unexpected need. 'Who was she?'

'Marie.' The sound of loss and regret pulsed through her. 'She was sixteen.'

'Like I was,' she breathed, absurdly glad to find some tenuous link between her teenaged self and his ghostly lover.

'Same age as you were,' he agreed. 'Only I didn't find someone else. She left me.'

'You met in hospital?' It was all beginning to fall into place.

He nodded, his fingers almost painfully tight but Polly didn't care, welcomed his grip, anchoring him to her. 'It's not like anywhere else,' he said. 'Everything is distilled down. You're defined by your illness but underneath? Underneath you're still a person, a teenager desperate to act out and find yourself, and the steroid bloating and the hair loss and the bruising and burns? None of it changes that. Marie and I met and we knew each other. Instantly.'

A shocking, unwanted jolt of jealousy hit her

and Polly swallowed it back. It was unworthy. Of her and of the story he was confiding in her.

'Tell me about her.' She wanted to know everything.

'She was understanding and acceptance. She was anger and rebellion and gallows humour. Just like me. It was…' he paused, searching for the right word '…intense. I don't know if we'd met in normal life if we'd have even liked each other. But then? Then she was all that I wanted, all that I needed. We were going to make it together or fail together.' He laughed softly, bitterly. 'The hubris of youth. But it didn't turn out the way we planned. I was so angry that she left me behind.'

'And now?'

'And now I am a decade older. That time is a memory, and Marie…' He swallowed. 'I don't even think of her day to day. I don't think of the boy I was. I took that time and I locked it away. I got well, I left Provence, left France, went away to college and I reinvented myself.'

'You're a survivor.'

She stopped and turned to face him. One hand was still held tightly in his; she allowed the other to drift up, to touch his cheek, to run along the defined line of his cheekbone and along the darkly stubbled jaw.

'You did what you had to do to survive. That makes you pretty darn amazing.'

He looked down at her, a pulse beating wildly in his cheek, the eyes almost black with pain. 'I forgot how to feel,' he said hoarsely. 'It hurt too much. Loss and pain and need. It was easier to smile and flirt and work and leave all that messy emotional stuff locked away. With Marie.'

'I know,' Polly whispered. She stared up at him. 'Emotions hurt.'

'Coming back, coming home, I can't forget. It's in every look, every word. My parents see me and they remember it all, all the hurt I caused them. And I see her, on every street corner, in every field. I see my broken promises.'

'You must have loved her very much.' Polly could hear the wistfulness in her voice and winced inwardly.

'Love?' He laughed softly. 'We were too young and fiery for love. I needed her, adored her, but love?' He looked right at her, gold flecks in his eyes mesmerising her. 'I don't know what love is either, Polly.'

She took a step towards him, eyes still fixed on his. The one small step had brought her into full contact, her chest pressed against his, hips against hips. She slid the hand cupping his face around his neck, allowing her fingers to run through the ends of his hair.

'Neither do I,' she said. 'I know want.' She stood on tiptoe and pressed a kiss on the pulse in his throat. He quivered. 'I know need.' Emboldened, she moved her mouth up and nipped his ear lobe. 'I know desire. Sometimes they're enough, they have to be enough.'

Her mouth moved to his, to drop a light butterfly kiss on the firm lips. She had only meant to comfort him, to take his mind off the past but one small step, three small kisses, three dangerous words shifted the mood, charged the air.

'Are they?' he asked, his eyes burning a question.

Polly couldn't answer, couldn't speak, could only nod as he continued to look hard into her eyes, into her soul.

She had no idea what he saw reflected there, all she knew was that she was boneless with desire, burning up with the unexpected, unwanted, but very real need pulsing through her, his body branding her, claiming her at every point they touched.

She didn't want him to think, didn't want any regrets, she just wanted him to hold her tight, wanted to taste him. She pulled her hand out of his, the momentary loss of contact chilling her until she slid her arm around his waist, working her hand under his T-shirt to feel the firm skin underneath. There under her fingers was the tattoo. She traced it from memory feeling him shudder under her touch.

'Goddammit, Polly,' he groaned. 'I'm trying...'

'Don't.'

It was all he needed. With a smothered cry of frustration, of need, he gave in, his arms pulling her in tight, one hand on her back, the other tangling in her hair.

He looked one last time, searching her face and whatever he saw there was enough because he lowered his mouth to hers. Claimed her. And she allowed it. Allowed herself to lose herself in his mouth, his hands, his hard, strong body. Today at least, in this moment, it was all she could give him.

And she would give all that he could take.

CHAPTER NINE

'OH, NO!'

Polly had barely waited until the plane had landed and the seat-belt light was switched off before she had pulled her phone out and switched it on.

Keeping busy. Avoiding conversation. Just as she had done all last night, all morning. Chatting to his mother, going on yet another guided tour with Claire, bathing Mathilde.

Avoiding conversation. Avoiding physical contact. Avoiding Gabe.

Gabe closed his eyes. It wasn't as if he had been trying to get her alone either.

It was all too *real*. The taste of her, cinnamon spicy and sweet. The softness of her hair, the warmth and smoothness of her skin. The exquisite torture of her hands, roaming over him as if she could learn him by heart...

He took a long, deep breath, willing away the

evocative memories. Willing away the urge to reach over, take her hands and draw her back to him. To lose himself in her again.

What had he been thinking? Necking like teenagers on a riverside path! Gabe couldn't remember the last time he had been content to hold and be held. To kiss, to touch with no expectation, no hurry to move on to the next stage. It wasn't just their admittedly exposed location. It was as if they were the teenage selves they had exhumed, armed with all that shy and explosive passion. No need to take it further. Content just to explore, to be.

No need to go further. Not then. And not since either.

It was probably all for the best. Every reason he had listed against getting involved with Polly still stood. Was valid. Even with the memory of the kiss thudding through him.

He opened his eyes and stared at the back of the airline seat. Yep, definitely all for the best.

'Honestly, does he never think?' Polly was still muttering as she glared at her phone as if it could answer her.

'Problems?' Gabe swung himself out of his

seat and opened the overhead locker to collect their bags.

'Grandfather.' It was said expressively. 'He wants to meet us at the house when we get back. My house. He's asked Raff. It hasn't even occurred to him that we might be tired.'

'Why should it?' Gabe swung Polly's neat overnight bag down and set it onto his seat. 'It's not even three in the afternoon. It's the middle of your working day. Besides, have you ever put tiredness before business before? It's not like he knows that you're pregnant.'

'That's not the point...'

'Polly.' He put his own bag onto the floor and turned to face her, taking in the dark circles under her eyes. She looked as if she had slept as well as he had. Was it the heat or the baby keeping her awake—or was she, like him, taunted by the memory of soft lips and caressing hands? Had she got out of bed several times, determined to creep down the landing hall to tap at his door only to fall back onto the bed unsure what to say, what to do?

'You need to tell him.'

She turned the full force of her glare on him but Gabe simply shouldered her bag and collected his own. 'It's time, Polly. Everything's looking good. You've accepted it. You need your family.'

She blinked, the long dark lashes falling in confusion. 'My family isn't like yours. We don't do unconditional love.'

'Then it's time you changed that,' he said and walked off along the nearly empty aisle.

She didn't speak to him again as they exited the airport and found their way to her car and this time, when Gabe held out his hand for her keys, she didn't protest, handing them over almost absent-mindedly. He had expected her to spend the journey back to Hopeford as she had every other moment that day, tapping on her laptop or phone or scribbling in her notebook, but she simply laid her head back on the headrest and stared out of the window.

It didn't take them long; the small airport was conveniently close to Hopeford and it was less than an hour later when Gabe turned into the narrow lane and parked outside the cottage. An old red Porsche was already parked there along with a Mercedes saloon.

'Great, the cavalry are already here.'

Gabe shot her a concerned look. Where was the

cool, collected Polly, in charge of everything and everyone? Where was the insistently questioning Polly, forcing him to face up to some unpalatable truths?

'Is that Raff's car? The vintage one?' Surely a mention of vintage cars would cheer her up.

'It was our father's. He got Daddy's car, I got Mummy's jewellery, the bits she left behind anyway. Never say that the Raffertys aren't conventional.'

She opened the door and slid out. 'Let's do this. Leave the bags, Gabe. We'll get them later.'

Gabe slowly exited the car and watched her. It was incredible seeing the way she breathed in, the mask slipping over her as she tilted her head up, straightened her back. She was every inch Polly Rafferty, CEO. On the outside at least.

He fell into step beside her but she didn't look at him as she marched up the small path that wound from the road through her flower-filled front garden to the wooden front door.

Twisting the handle, she made a face as the door opened with no need for a key. 'Hello,' she called as she pushed it open. 'If you're burglars then there isn't anything worth taking. If it's Raff how the hell did you get in?'

'Ah, that's my fault. I abused my position as your concierge service but I thought you would prefer to come home to a prepared dinner and a settled-in grandparent.' A woman with a heart-shaped face, wavy red-gold hair and the greenest eyes Gabe had ever seen came through from the kitchen, smiling a little shyly. 'Hi, Polly. I'm so sorry I haven't been round before today. Good trip?'

Polly stood stock-still for a moment and Gabe felt her take an audible deep breath as if steeling herself before she moved forward, her face wreathed in smiles. 'Clara! I should have known. It's so good to see you. Let me see…' She grabbed Clara's left hand and stared at the antique emerald ring on her third finger.

'I know it's customary to say congratulations but as Raff's twin I can't square it with my conscience if I don't first say *run*. I lived with him for eighteen years and you are far too good for him.'

Clara was glowing with happiness. 'It's too late.

Summer would never forgive me. He's promised to take her to two theme parks in Florida this year.'

Polly shook her head. 'That's my brother. He always targets the weak spot! Congratulations, Clara. I hope you will be very happy. Have you met Gabe yet? Gabe, this is Clara, my brother's fiancée.'

'No, we haven't met but I know Raff, of course. Please accept my felicitations.' Gabe shook her hand warmly and smiled down into the green eyes.

'Polly, I am so sorry,' Clara whispered. 'I said you would probably be too tired for a meeting now, and the last thing you would want was your house invaded, but your grandfather was so insistent. I got Dad to make some food I can heat up, just a lasagne and salad, and Sue will clean it all up tomorrow so, really, all you have to do is eat.'

Polly didn't know how she would have managed without Clara's concierge service to manage her life over the last three years; she had never been more grateful for her friend's organisational powers.

'That's okay.' Polly gave Clara's hand a squeeze.

'But I hope you're sticking around. You're part of the family now. Where is everyone?'

Clara smiled back at her friend. 'Thanks, Polly. They're in the sitting room. Oh, and just to warn you before you go in, your grandmother is there as well.'

'What? With Grandfather? In the same room? Good God, thank goodness I don't have any priceless antiques.'

Polly led the way through the low-beamed door into the pretty sitting room. Gabe was so used to seeing the house empty it was a shock to find the room full of people. Charles Rafferty was ensconced on the straight-backed armchair by the unlit fire, his despised stick by his side. A white-haired, regal-looking woman with an unmistakeable look of the Rafferty twins in her straight nose and shrewd blue eyes was sitting on the sofa talking to Raff while a dark-haired girl of ten or so was lying on the floor whispering softly to Mr Simpkins as he purred around her hand.

'This is quite the welcoming committee.' Polly looked calm and collected as she walked in. 'Hello, Grandmother.' She went over to the sofa and kissed the older lady's cheek. 'Raff.' A cool

nod at her brother. 'Grandfather.' Another nod.
'Hi, Summer, how was Australia?'

'Polly!' The girl scrambled to her feet. 'Do you
know you're going to be my aunt?'

'I do.' Polly stepped over and gave her a quick
hug. 'My first niece. I'm looking forward to it.'

There was an ache at the back of Gabe's throat
as he watched her dance so awkwardly around her
family. She was right: he kept his at arm's length
but it didn't matter. They would always be there,
love him, have a space for him. Nothing he could
do would provoke this kind of cold and formal
reception.

He *should* go home more often. Talk to his papa
about his future plans. Help out a little.

'Sorry for gatecrashing, Pol.' Raff was twin-
kling up at his sister. 'Grandfather insisted.'

'Clara explained. It's okay, of course you're all
welcome but there's not much I can tell you today.
Gabe and I haven't had an opportunity to pull our
research together, although after seeing what Natalie is doing with the software on a smaller scale
I have to say I'm very close to being completely
convinced if we can make the numbers add up...'

'This isn't about Rafferty's,' her grandfather interrupted and Gabe could feel the shock reverberate through Polly as her cheeks whitened and she took a step closer to her grandfather's chair.

'Not about Rafferty's? Are you ill? I knew you should have stepped down earlier!'

'Charles isn't ill, at least, no worse than he was before the angina attack.' Polly's grandmother spoke calmly and Polly held her stare, looking for and apparently finding reassurance.

'Then what?'

'Polly dear, your grandfather and I are going to remarry.'

Polly looked down the wooden table at her family and resisted the urge to rub her eyes. It was ironic, just last night she would have given anything to have her family congregated in her kitchen the way the Beaufils did, all eating together.

And here they were. Sure, it was a little more formal, a tad more awkward than in the Provence farmhouse. Summer was unusually tongue-tied and Gabe evidently embarrassed about being caught up in the family drama. Clara...

Clara only had eyes for Raff and he for her.

A hollow pit opened up in Polly's stomach.

What would it be like for someone to look at her like that? As if she were the answer to every question? To every prayer.

Yesterday with Gabe she had come close. Close to letting him in. Colour flushed her cheeks as she remembered. She had almost begged him. No wonder he couldn't meet her eyes.

'Not hungry, Polly?' Clara looked pointedly at Polly's almost untouched plate.

'Sorry, Clara. Please don't tell your father. It was delicious as always. I'm just tired, I guess.' Without meaning to, Polly allowed her eyes to wander over to Gabe, somehow at the head of the table. Of *her* table. He looked completely at ease, mid-conversation with her grandfather, long fingers playing on the stem of his wine glass.

Fingers that just yesterday had been playing on her skin.

Polly shivered. How could a kiss be that sensual? More erotic than the most practised love-making?

What would it have been like if they had been somewhere more private? If they had gone further? If she had been able to explore that tattoo the way she had burned to, tracing it with the tip of her finger. With kisses. With her tongue, slick on salty skin.

She clenched her hands, allowing the nails to dig into her palms. She was at dinner, for goodness' sake. With her grandparents.

With her brother.

With Gabe…

He looked up, with that sixth sense he seemed to possess whenever she thought about him, eyes dark and intent.

'We should celebrate,' he said abruptly. 'Two engagements require champagne.'

'Yes, of course.' She should have thought of that. It was her house after all. And she was the only one without news to celebrate. Publicly at least. 'There's a couple of bottles out back.'

'I'll get them.' He pushed his chair back and disappeared into the pantry, reappearing with one of the bottles that had been chilling in the old stone cold room.

'Summer, *ma chérie*, could you go to the cupboard there and get me six of the long glasses? *Oui*, clever girl.' He flashed his warmest smile at the small girl as Summer proudly put the glasses on the table and Polly pushed her still-full wine glass to one side.

It had been easier to accept the glass and not touch it rather than face any questions. Gabe was right, she needed to say something. But how?

With an expert twist Gabe loosed the cork and began to pour the bubble-filled amber liquid into the first glass, handing the first to her grandmother and the second to Clara. When every glass had been filled and handed around every face turned expectantly to Polly.

Of course. This was her role. Head of the family firm.

She got to her feet, trying to drag her thoughts back to the here and now, to the unexpected news that had greeted her return home.

'So there are two engagements to celebrate,' she said, keeping her voice as steady as she could. Raff and Clara were smiling up at her, her grandparents regarding her with more warmth than she had seen from them in a long time.

Her eyes flickered to Gabe. His eyes were fixed on her, expression inscrutable.

'I know my job involves looking for trends and seeing what lies ahead so all I can say is that

thank goodness I don't run a dating agency because I didn't predict either of these. But that
doesn't mean that I'm not truly happy for you all.
Clara, you've been my closest friend in Hopeford.'

So close that I haven't seen you since I returned,
a little voice whispered but Polly ignored it.

'I know how much Raff loves you and I know he
will do everything he can to make you happy—
and when Raff sets his mind to something he usually achieves it!

'And Grandfather, Grandmother. Thank you for
raising Raff and me. I know it wasn't easy, that we
weren't easy. I know it put a strain on you. I'm just
glad you've found your way back together after
thirteen years. You're the most formidable team
I know. So.' She held her glass high. 'To the Raffertys. Congratulations.'

'The Raffertys,' they chorused, glasses held to
hers before they sipped.

Polly put her glass down thankfully.

'Aunty Polly,' Summer's voice rang out clearly.
'Why aren't you drinking yours?'

Every eye turned to Polly and she sank back
into her seat, instinctively looking over at Gabe
for help.

But he just sat there.

'You didn't drink any wine either.' Raff sounded accusatory.

For goodness' sake, wasn't a girl allowed to not drink? It wasn't as if she were a lush!

But maybe Gabe was right. They had to know soon enough and although a big announcement hadn't been her plan maybe it would be better to tell them all in one fell swoop. Like ripping off a plaster.

Polly took a breath, feeling the air shudder through her.

'I have a little announcement of my own. This isn't quite how I wanted to do it...' she looked around the table, desperate for some reassurance '...but I suppose there isn't an easy way so I'm just going to say it. I'm pregnant.'

'That's great, Polly.' But Clara's voice was lost as both Raff and her grandfather sprang to their feet.

'Pregnant?'

'You'll marry her, of course!' Her grandfather was glaring at Gabe.

'What do you mean, pregnant?'

So much for extending the celebrations.

The noise levels rose. Polly couldn't think, didn't know which angry, accusatory face to answer first. 'Stop it!' She had risen to her feet as well, hands crashing down onto the table, rattling the crockery and silverware.

'Come on, Summer, let's go for a walk.' Clara threw her an apologetic glance as she shepherded her daughter from the table. 'We'll talk later, Polly. It's great news. Raff?' Her eyes bored into her fiancé, an implicit warning. 'I'll see you at home.'

Raff sank back into his seat. 'Sorry, Polly. It was just, it was a shock.'

Charles Rafferty wasn't so easily cowed. He was still on his feet and glaring over at Gabe. 'Well?' he demanded.

'Grandfather!' Polly said sharply. 'For goodness' sake. You are not some medieval knight, much as you might wish it, and I am *not* some dishonoured damsel to be married off to avoid a scandal. This is a good thing and it has *nothing* to do with Gabe.'

Maybe she had put too much emphasis on the 'nothing', she conceded as the Frenchman whitened, and added: 'I've only known him a few weeks.'

'Then whose is it?'

'Mine,' she said firmly. 'This is the twenty-first century, I am thirty-one and I am quite capable of doing this alone.'

'Yes, dear, we know how independent you are.' Her grandmother sounded like a dowager duchess from the turn of the last century. 'But what your grandfather means is who fathered it? Unless you went to one of those clinics,' she said a little doubtfully.

If only she had! That would be so much easier to admit.

'Someone I met travelling.' She held up her hand. 'I don't know his surname. Obviously if I had foreseen this I would have exchanged business cards but I didn't. So it's up to me. And you, if you want to be involved.'

'Of course we do, dear, don't be so melodramatic.'

But her grandmother's words were negated by her grandfather's expression. Shock, disapproval, horror, disgust passing over his face in rapid but sickening procession.

'A granddaughter of mine? Besmirching the family name with some dreadlocked backpacker?

I told you to get married, Polly. I told you to set-tle down...'

'With respect, *monsieur*, that's enough.' Now Gabe was on his feet. 'Polly has done nothing wrong. It may not be your preferred path for her but she is going to be a great mother—and a great CEO.'

'A single mother in charge of Rafferty's?' Charles Rafferty huffed out a disparaging laugh. 'I thought you had more sense than that, Beau-fils. As for you, Polly, I knew letting you take over was a mistake. I should have stuck with my gut instinct.'

The blood rushed from her cheeks and her knees weakened. He'd admitted it. He didn't want her. Her appointment, her career was nothing but a mistake in his eyes.

'Clara's a single mother,' Raff said. His voice was mild but there was a steely glint in his eyes. 'At least she was. Polly, I'm sorry, you...' He rubbed his jaw, the blue eyes rueful. 'You sur-prised me but you're not alone. I hope you know that. Clara and I are right here.' Polly nodded, numb inside, her eyes returning to her grandfa-ther, still standing up, still glaring.

'You two always did stick together,' he said. 'It doesn't change anything. It's hard enough for any working mother to be at the top, impossible for a woman on her own. It's not old-fashioned, it's common sense.'

'There are plenty of single parents at Rafferty's, men and women.' Gabe's voice was soft but it cut through the tense air, drawing all the attention away from Polly, and she folded herself back into her chair, clasping her hands together to keep them from trembling.

'The only person, *monsieur*, who sees a problem here is you. Which is ironic because if you had seen her worth earlier, if you hadn't pushed her away, then maybe she wouldn't be in this position. You need to think very carefully about how you treat and value your granddaughter before you lose her for ever—and the great-grandchild she is carrying.'

Charles Rafferty paled and Polly and Raff exchanged a concerned glance as he sat down heavily in his chair. His tongue wasn't weakened though. 'I thought we had established that this has nothing to do with you.'

Gabe didn't quail under the withering tone.

'*Non?* Who held her hair when she was sick? Who sat with her during the first scan? I didn't ask to be involved but she has no one else. You make it quite clear that she can't come to you.'

Charles Rafferty gasped, a shuddering intake of breath, and Polly was back on her feet. Before she could move round to him Raff had passed their grandfather a glass of water and her grandmother had moved round to him, her usually aloof expression one of concern.

This was all getting horribly out of hand. 'Gabe!' How dared he? How dared he try and explain away her actions? Interfere? 'A word? In private?'

Still trembling but now more with anger than with shock, she led him outside. Normally her garden was one of her favourite spots with shady, hidden spaces and a stream running across the bottom. Today it was just somewhere convenient.

'How dare you talk to my grandfather like that? What the hell do you think you're doing?'

His mouth hardened into a thin line. 'Standing up for you.'

The nerve of him! 'I didn't ask you to.'

His eyes narrowed contemptuously. '*Non?* I must have misunderstood the beseeching look you threw me when you sat there mute as your family shouted at you.'

'I didn't, at least I didn't mean for you to attack my grandfather! I don't need help. I am quite capable of standing up for myself.'

'*Oui*, keep telling yourself that.'

The words were thrown at her, sharp as arrows, and she quailed under them. 'What do you mean by that?'

'What I say. You tell me, you tell yourself that you don't need anything—anyone.' His eyes had darkened with an unbearable sympathy. 'But you're still just a little girl tugging at her grandfather's sleeve wanting attention. Without it, you allow yourself to be nothing.'

Polly hadn't known words could hurt before, not physically, but each of Gabe's words was like a sharp stab in her chest. 'How dare you...?'

'He rules the board, he rules you. He uses his health to keep you quiet and his disapproval to keep you tame. When he said you couldn't take over, did you stay to fight, to prove him wrong? No, you ran away.'

How had this happened? How had the passion

and need of yesterday turned into these cruel words, ripping her apart?

'I couldn't stay. You know that.'

'You *chose* not to stay.' He laughed, not unkindly but the tone didn't matter. The unbearable sympathy on his face didn't matter. The words were all that mattered and they were harsh.

They were true. He had seen inside her and he was stripping her to the bone.

'You were quick enough to label me a coward, to judge me, but you know what, Polly? You were right when you said we were just the same. We define ourselves through work because without it? What is there? Who are we? Nothing.'

Polly stood there looking at him. She had thought that she knew him. Knew the feel of his mouth, the taste of him. The way the muscles on his shoulders moved, the play of them under her hands.

She'd thought that she understood him. That he might be coming to understand her. Maybe he did, all too well. She was defenceless.

'Get out,' she said, proud when her voice didn't waver. When the threatened tears didn't fall. 'Get out and leave me alone.'

He stood there for a long moment looking at her. She didn't move, didn't waver.

'You need people in your corner, Polly,' he said softly. 'People who will be there for you no matter what. Pick wisely.'

And he was gone.

Tears trembled behind her eyes but she blinked them back. *You don't cry, remember?*

She took a deep breath, almost doubling over at the unexpected ache in her chest, the raw, exposed pain and grief, like Prometheus torn open, awaiting the eagles. She had lost everything. Her grandfather. Gabe.

But no. She straightened, her hand splayed open on her still-flat stomach. Not everything.

She could do this. She could absolutely do this alone. Gabe was wrong. In every way.

Slowly she turned and walked back to the kitchen. Her family were at the table where she had left them and she was relieved to see colour in her grandfather's cheeks. Maybe she could fix this. She had to fix something.

'I'm sorry about what Gabe said.' She took her seat and picked up her water glass, relieved that her hands had stopped shaking enough for her to drink. 'He was out of line.'

She bowed her head and waited for more reproach and anger to be heaped on her.

'Charles.' Her grandmother spoke sharply and her grandfather leant forward, reaching for one of Polly's hands.

She couldn't remember the last time he had touched her first; she was usually the one bestowing a dutiful kiss on his cheek.

It felt comforting to have her hand in his. Unbidden, Gabe's words sprang into her mind. *You're still just a little girl tugging at her grandfather's sleeve.*

'I'm sorry, Polly.' Charles Rafferty's voice was a little wavery, his speech unusually slow and Polly's chest tightened with love and fear. 'I was shocked and I reacted badly. I said some terrible things and I hope you can forgive me, my dear.'

An apology? From the formidable Mr Rafferty? 'I'm sorry too,' she said, squeezing his fingers. When had they got so frail? 'I should have told you earlier. I needed time to process everything, to deal with it all, but I should have come to you.'

'You always were independent,' he said.

Was she? Polly wondered. Or did she just want to be thought that way? Was Gabe right?

'I didn't mean for this to happen.' She looked at her grandparents, pleading for them to understand. They might not be perfect but they were the only parental figures she had. She needed them. 'I was lost and met someone as lonely as me. He was nice, a teacher in Copenhagen and recently divorced. I *have* tried to track him down but with no picture or surname the private investigator wasn't hopeful. He gave it a week and then told me to save my money. You know how much I missed Daddy. I hate the fact that my baby will grow up not knowing his or her father.'

'Polly dearest.' Her grandmother was suspiciously bright eyed. 'Did Gabriel say something about a scan? I don't suppose there's a picture…'

A glimmer of something that felt a little like hope skimmed through Polly. 'There is a picture,' she said. 'Would you like to see it?'

CHAPTER TEN

'IT DIDN'T LOOK this dark on the tin.' Polly stood back from the wall and stared at the first splash of paint. 'I'm not intending to raise a baby Goth.'

'It'll be lighter when it dries.' Clara joined her and looked doubtfully at the wall. 'I hope. Are you sure you don't want me to find somebody to do it for you?'

'No, I am doing it all myself. My baby, my walls, my botch paint job in deepest purple.' Polly glanced at the tin. 'It's supposed to be lilac lace.'

'You *can* outsource some of the work, you know. To Raff or to me. I do special discounts for family…'

'I might consider outsourcing the actual birth part. That looks a little scary.' The books Clara had given her were piled high on the chest of drawers in the sunny room at the back of the house Polly had decided on for the nursery. After a quick flick through the graphic words and even more graphic pictures Polly had put them aside vowing not to go anywhere near them again.

There was some protection in ignorance.

'Sorry, Polly, there are some things even you can't delegate away.' Clara dipped her paintbrush in the deep colour and began to apply it to the walls in sweeping strokes. 'Talking of delegation, have you spoken to Gabe?' She sounded disinterested but the sly glance she slid Polly belied the light tone.

'I've sat in meetings with him.'

'Let me rephrase that. Have you had a conversation with Gabe, just the two of you, that hasn't involved spreadsheets, budgets and forecasts?'

'That would be a negative.'

Clara added a bit more paint to her brush. 'Polly,' she said slowly. 'We've known each other for a while and I like to think that although we've never touched on anything really deep we're good friends.'

Polly bit her lip. Truth was Clara was her only friend. And yet she knew so little about the woman who was going to marry her twin. 'Of course we are, and I am delighted you're going to be my sister.'

'And the aunt of the lucky future possessor of these walls,' Clara agreed. 'So I hope you don't mind me prying a little bit but what is going on with you and Gabe?'

That was easy enough to answer. 'We're colleagues.'

'That's all?' Clara persisted.

Polly sighed and put her paintbrush down on the newspaper she'd spread over the furniture, before sliding onto the floor and hugging her knees. 'We kissed. Twice. Well, once was an accident.'

Not the other. No, the other had been wonderfully intentional.

'Don't you hate those accidental kisses?' Clara murmured, laughter in her voice.

Now she had started confiding Polly couldn't bear to stop. It was almost a relief to let the words spill out. 'We talked. Spent some time together.' It didn't sound much. Not the bare, bald facts. 'He was there when I needed him. And he was brilliant; patient and helpful and understanding. He's good to work with too, sparky and innovative and pushes me...' Her voice trailed off.

'Sounds good.' Clara was still painting. It was

easier talking to her back than to have to face her, see concern or sympathy in her eyes.

'It was. I've only known him a couple of weeks but I thought maybe we had a connection.' Polly pulled at her ponytail. 'It's stupid, hormones playing up. I should have known better. Neither of us are looking for anything, want anything. In a different time or place maybe we could have had a thing. But the timing was off.'

And she didn't want a 'thing'. Not any more. Not with anyone. Especially not with Gabe.

She'd spent her twenties valuing her independence, her ability to walk away. It didn't seem such an achievement any more.

Clara painted another streak of colour onto the wall and stood back to assess the effect. Her voice was still light, conversational. 'You don't need to be looking to find it. I wasn't, Raff wasn't. We tried hard not to fall in love but it was too strong.'

Love? Polly swallowed hard, her heartbeat speeding up. 'Who said anything about love?'

'No one. Yet. But you said yourself there's a connection; he pushes you, understands you— and the kisses were good enough to make your voice go hazy just thinking about them. Even if one *was* an accident.'

Clara put her paintbrush down beside Polly's and slid into place beside her. 'It might not be love, Polly, not yet. But it sounds pretty close to me. I don't know why you've pushed him away, nor why he has let you. But isn't it worth trying swallowing your pride?'

'I miss him,' Polly admitted.

But it was more than that. She'd lived alone in this big old house for so long, had never felt lonely in it before. But now his absence was in every room.

It was ridiculous; he'd hardly spent any time there as it was.

It was the same at work. Sometimes she would look up from her desk and glance over at the empty space where his desk had so briefly sat. It was so quiet without him typing loudly, his continuous conversations. The room so still without his pacing up and down. She would listen jealously for some mention of his name, to find out who he was flirting with this week.

But the staff grapevine was quiet.

And she *was* lonely. Raff and Clara were doing

their best, almost overwhelming her with dinners and visits, trying to include her in everything. And she appreciated it, she really did. Only they were so very together.

It made her feel her solitary state even more.

She had never cared about being alone before. Or allowed herself to admit it.

'He took you to the hospital, helped when you were sick, what makes you think he doesn't want more? Have you asked him?' Clara was pushing but Polly didn't mind. The last few weeks, his last words had been going round and round in her head like an overactive carousel until she was so giddy she couldn't think. This was her opportunity to get it all straight.

To get over it.

'I don't need to. He's…' Polly searched for the right word. 'He's complex, Clara. He has this amazing family.' She could hear the wistfulness in her own voice and cringed. 'They're really supportive and loving, like yours if you multiplied your family by three, the noise level by ten, added in a host of toddlers and moved to France.'

'Just like my family, then.'

'Yours was the happiest, most together family I knew until I met the Beaufils,' Polly admitted.

'So he has the family you always wanted,' Clara said shrewdly. 'I still don't see the problem.'

'He was ill, really ill in his teens and it nearly killed his parents.' Polly winced as she pictured the pain in his dark eyes. 'I don't know whether he really blames them for caring so much or himself for causing so much pain. I think it's a mixture of both. Throw in a first love who died in her teens and you have one emotionally mixed-up man.'

'We all have our scars, but most of us are redeemable. For the right person.'

'That's just it.' Clara had got it. 'I'm *not* the right person, Clara. Gabe needs someone who understands him, someone with the patience to wait for him, to help him. Me? I have a business to run, a baby on the way. I have no idea how a functioning family works. I can't help him! He deserves better.'

Clara didn't say anything for a long moment and then she got up and picked up the paintbrush. 'It's a lot, I agree,' she said. 'But you've never backed down from anything daunting before. If you think you and he have a chance, if you think it might, could be love, then you should go for it. But, Polly, if you're backing down out of fear, then you're letting yourself down and you're letting Gabe down. Be sure before you let him walk away.'

He still had a key in his pocket but using it just didn't feel right. Not with her car parked outside and the windows flung open.

A part of Gabe had hoped that Polly was out, working maybe or with her brother, that he could have nipped in, gathered his stuff and left again leaving no trace.

Taking a deep breath, he pressed the doorbell. How hard could this be? After all, they saw each other every day at work. They sent emails, held meetings. It was all fine.

Polite. Formal. Fine.

There was a pause and then the sound of light footsteps running down the stairs before the door was pulled open.

'I left it open for you...oh!' Polly stepped back, her eyes huge with surprise. 'You're not Clara.'

'*Non,*' he agreed.

'She was just here, helping me paint and popped

out for sandwiches so I thought, I assumed...' Her voice trailed off.

'Paint?' That made sense, he thought as his gaze travelled up her despite his best intentions to stay cool and focused. Bare feet, long tanned legs in a pair of cut-off denim shorts. Who would have thought the elegant Polly Rafferty even owned such disreputable-looking garments, fraying and paint splattered?

Her vest top was falling off one shoulder, revealing a delicate lilac bra strap.

Lilac. The colour he had bought her. It might even be the same set. His breath hitched, his heartbeat speeding up, blood pounding around his body in a relentless march.

No. He dragged his mind back to the matter at hand. They weren't on those kinds of terms, not any more.

They had almost got in too deep; he'd allowed her in too deep. Thank goodness Polly had seen sense.

Her hands tightened on the door. 'I'm decorating the baby's room purple, to go with the bunting. Only it's a little darker than I thought, more bordello than nursery.'

'It might lighten when it dries.' He shifted his weight onto the other foot. Such a non-conversation. As if they were mere acquaintances.

'That's the hope,' Polly said.

She still hadn't asked him in.

'I just wanted to return your key and get the last of my things.'

'Oh.' Her eyelashes dropped, veiling her eyes. 'Of course, come in.'

She opened the door fully, stepping aside as she did so. 'Is your flat fixed?'

Gabe grimaced. 'Unfortunately not. The underground cinema and gym is proving most expensive for my oligarch neighbour. He's still paying hotel bills for at least twenty people.'

'Including you?'

He shrugged. 'There's a gym. It's convenient for work. No more trains.'

'That's good.'

Gabe stepped over the threshold and stopped, unwanted regret and nostalgia twisting his stomach. The scent of fresh flowers mixed with beeswax and that spicy scent Polly favoured, a dark cinnamon, hit him. It smelled like home.

Only it wasn't. Not any more. It never really had been.

She was right to have pushed him away. What did he have to offer? Financial security? She had her own. No, what Polly needed was emotional security.

The one thing he couldn't offer.

She deserved it. Deserved more than a coward who spent his life hiding from his own family so that he didn't have to face up to the possibility of losing them. Of letting them down.

'I don't have much.' He needed to pack, to get out and leave the memories behind. Start afresh.

She turned to him, one hand twisting her ponytail, the other playing with the frayed cotton on her shorts. 'Gabe, I'm sorry,' she said.

What? 'No, I should apologise to you.' He squeezed his eyes shut. 'I was harsh. Unfair.'

'You were right.' She exhaled. 'You just gave me some home truths. I didn't want to hear them, to admit them. That doesn't stop them being true.' She huffed out a laugh. 'There doesn't seem to be a warning sign with us, does there? We just say whatever is in our heads and damn the consequences. I've never been so honest with any-one before.'

'No, me neither.'

'I'm not sure I like it.' She moved away towards the kitchen. 'Would you like a coffee?'

Gabe had intended to make a quick exit but he recognised the offer for what it was: a peace of-fering. 'Do you have decaf?'

'A month ago I would have laughed in your face but pregnancy does strange things to a woman. I have decaf and a whole selection of herbal teas, each more vile than the rest.'

'I could make you a smoothie,' he suggested and laughed, the tension broken by the horror in her eyes.

'Spinach and beetroot and those horrid seeds? I'm pregnant, not crazy.' She busied herself at the expensive coffee machine and Gabe leant on the counter, idly looking at the papers there. One let-ter caught his eye and he read a few lines before realising it was personal. He pushed it away just as she looked over.

Awkward, as if he had been caught purposely snooping, he gestured at the letter. 'You have a hospital appointment?'

'Yes. Clara's agreed to accompany me.'

His duties were well and truly over. He was free, to concentrate on work, to train for the Alpine triathlon in the autumn. To live his life the way he wanted it with no interruptions.

It was all going back to normal.

Polly walked back over, a steaming cup of coffee in her hand. 'Gabe.' She put the coffee down next to him. 'I really need to thank you. For everything.'

He shrugged. 'I was here. Anyone would have done the same.'

'Maybe, but you stepped up, more than once. You didn't have to. Not just with the practical stuff.'

She pulled up a stool and sank onto it, pulling the letter from the hospital over towards her, folding it over and over. 'I've been thinking a lot lately. About what I want from my life. I guess the pregnancy would have forced me to make some changes anyway but it's not just that. You *made* me think. About the kind of person, the kind of parent I want to be. My work, Rafferty's, is incredibly important, that won't change. But it's not enough. It shouldn't be enough. I don't want to turn into a female version of Grandfather, putting the business before family, before happiness.

'I'm going to have a baby.' Her eyes were shining. Gabe had seen Polly experience a whole range of emotions about the pregnancy: shock, grief, acceptance. But not joy like this. Not before today. 'And I want that baby to have a family. I think, deep down, there's a bit of me that's always wanted your kind of family. Ironic, isn't it? When you find them too much?'

'Swap?' he offered.

'In a heartbeat.' She folded the paper again. 'I can't conjure up parents and a partner for the baby, but I want him or her to grow up with love and laughter and security. Clara and Raff will help, if I let them. And I will. I need to start letting people in. So thank you. For helping me realise that.'

'You're welcome.' The words almost stuck in his throat.

She smiled at him but there was sadness in her eyes. 'I just hope you find what you're looking for,' she said.

Gabe wanted to make some flippant comment but she was right. They *were* always honest with each other, no matter what the consequences. 'I'm not looking for much. Another year healthy? Another goal achieved?' It didn't sound like much but it was all he had.

'I wish I could have helped you, the way you've helped me. It's not that I don't want to try, arrogant as that sounds, but I do. I like you, Gabe.' The colour flared on her cheeks.

Gabe wanted to speak out. To tell her that she had helped, that with her he had finally confronted memories locked away for too long.

To tell her how much he liked her too. That he lay awake at night replaying every single moment of that kiss, his skin heating where she had touched him.

But he didn't know how to.

Polly took a deep breath. 'I don't know what love is, not really. But I think we were close. At least, I was close. The closest I've ever been. But I have the baby to think of, the security I have promised it. Right now, it needs me to be putting it first, to be strong for it.'

She reached over and took his hand, her fingers soft in his. He curled his hand round hers, holding them tight and she raised his hand to her lips, dropping a kiss onto his knuckles. 'My mother didn't put us first. Or second or anywhere. Her need for love came before anything else. I guess I overcompensated, desperate to show the world that I didn't need anyone. That I wasn't like her. Now I wonder if maybe I took it too far. But now isn't the time to worry about that. I can't put myself first, not any more.'

'No.' What else was there to say?

'I do believe that there's someone out there who'll show you that life isn't a challenge or a goal, it's a blessing.' She closed her eyes, blinking back a tear. 'I have to admit I'm a little jealous of that someone.' Her voice was so low he hardly heard the words. 'Maybe you'll do it on your own. You're strong enough, goodness knows. The burdens you bear. The misplaced guilt.'

'I'm happy for you, really I am. But I'm fine.' He tried to smile. 'I don't need fixing.'

So much for honesty. He was utterly broken and they both knew it.

Breathe. Breathe. Breathe. It wasn't easy training for an Alpine triathlon in a busy, flat city like London. It was a particularly gruelling trial, a lake swim followed by a ninety-kilometre cycle-ride and a full marathon run. Although the trails didn't go too high up into the Tyrolean mountains it was a hilly course.

Just finishing wasn't an option. He wanted a winning time.

There was nothing better than pushing his body to its limits. Proving he was no longer at its mercy, that his mind was in control at all times.

Control. He'd lost it the past few weeks. It was time to regain it.

Gabe stopped, leaning against a tree, and took a swig of water. It didn't take long for fitness levels to drop. For an easy ten-kilometre jog to become a challenge.

He just needed to get his rhythm back, to regain that blissful state where all he knew was the thud of his feet, the beating of his heart.

Instead he ran to a soundtrack of Polly's voice, sad, resigned, defeated. *I like you.*

And he'd said? He'd said nothing. Because what could he say?

I wish I could have helped you, the way you've helped me.

Of course she did. She was an achiever. Polly

Rafferty didn't like to leave tasks unfinished, a list unticked. She'd wanted to see him reconciled with his family, the past dealt with.

She was getting her happy ever after, she just wanted the same for him.

It was a shame life just wasn't that tidy.

Gabe set off again, wiping the perspiration off his forehead as he increased the tempo. He didn't need a happy ever after. He didn't deserve one.

But she did.

She deserved the whole damn fairy tale. Paris at her feet.

He just hoped that she would meet someone who recognised that.

The thought reverberated around his head, the echo getting louder and louder.

Someone else.

His stomach clenched and Gabe skidded to a stop, bending forward to alleviate the cramp, hand on his side.

No, he didn't want that for her at all.

Oh, how he wished he could be that altruistic, that selfless, that he could put her needs first. But he didn't think he could survive watching her laugh with another man, talking cars with another man, showing off vintage designs to another man, fired up as she planned business and strategy with another man.

Kissing another man.

Raising her child with another man.

And there would be someone else. For all her brave talk about going it alone, there would be. She might not have fallen in love in the past but she'd had partners whenever she needed them. How long before the new, softer Polly was snapped up? Opened up her heart to some lucky man?

They'd be queuing around the block.

And he was just going to let them?

Gabe straightened up, oblivious to the people walking around him, the sighs and tuts from commuters unwilling to step around a human being in their well-trodden path.

Of course he wasn't going to let them!

I like you, she had said. More than once. What must it have taken for the proud Polly Rafferty to say those words? And he hadn't reacted. Hadn't told her.

That he liked her too.

It was time he did.

If Polly wanted to have the whole white-picket-fence dream while running the world's most famous department store then she was going to need the best by her side.

And Gabe had always liked a challenge.

CHAPTER ELEVEN

'GOOD MORNING, RACHEL.'

Polly smiled at her assistant. Rachel had done her job beautifully. Unable to bear some big announcement of her pregnancy, Polly had, instead, confided in her PA. The news had spread around the store in less than a day, just as Polly had known it would.

At some point she would have to have a word with the gossip-loving woman about confidentiality and discretion. But not yet, not when she had just used Rachel to her advantage.

'Good morning, Miss Rafferty. There is a mint tea on your desk and Chef says that he has a summer fruit compote and a breakfast omelette for you this morning.'

It was surprising—and rather sweet—how many of her staff had taken the news of her pregnancy and turned it into a project. The kitchen sent up nutritious meals three times a day and were hope fully awaiting outlandish cravings so that they could rise to whatever challenge she set.

The make-up department manager had put together an entire basket of pre-natal oils, creams and bath salts and was sourcing and testing the very best in post-natal and baby unguents. As for the personal shoppers, not only were they putting aside more clothes than triplets could easily get through, they were also ensuring she would be the chicest mother-to-be in London.

Polly had always felt respected rather than liked—she had encouraged it. This new two-way process was a little disconcerting. But she was rather enjoying the interest and attention. It didn't feel as intrusive as she had feared, more warm and friendly.

Only Gabe was nowhere to be seen. He seemed to be constantly in meetings although he sent detailed emails and was obviously working as hard as ever. It wasn't hard to deduce that he was avoiding her.

She shouldn't have used words like love.

But somehow Polly couldn't bring herself to feel regret or embarrassment. She'd tried.

A little at least.

'Oh, Miss Rafferty, there's been a change to your afternoon appointment. The one with the web developer?'

'Has he postponed?'

Up to now Polly had left all the details about the possible new website with Gabe, but she wanted to check some final budgets and meet the developer herself before making the final recommendation.

Finding a mutually convenient date had been problematic—and now he couldn't make it? She hoped this wasn't a portent of his professional reliability.

'He's stuck in Paris and asked if you would mind going there instead?'

'To Paris?' Polly echoed. 'That's...'

'Less time to get to than Edinburgh,' Rachel said, putting a pile of papers onto the desk. 'I've booked you onto the noon Eurostar so a taxi will be here to take you to St Pancras for eleven. A car will collect you at the other end.'

Rachel looked a little anxious. 'I have done the right thing, haven't I? It's just you told me to use my initiative more and I know you want to talk to him yourself before making a final decision...'

'No, you did right. As you say it's quicker than

Edinburgh.' Polly scooped up the pile of papers, including her passport, she kept it at work for just this reason, and retreated into her office.

Sorry, Mummy, looks like I won't be keeping my word after all, she thought. But maybe this is a good thing. Demystify Paris as part of her new start.

Baby steps.

It was so comfortable in Business Class that Polly realised with a jump that she had almost nodded off. *I think I preferred the nausea to the tiredness,* she thought as she jolted back to awareness when the train braked, the papers still unread on the table in front of her, her laptop reverted to sleep mode. There were times when she eyed the couch in her office longingly, desperate to stretch out and just close her eyes.

Until she remembered Gabe sprawled out. The firm toned lines of his body, the tree spiralling up his back.

The couch seemed a lot less safe then.

Polly pulled her mind back to the present. She had enough to do without daydreaming and dwelling on the past, including finding her way around a totally strange city. Paris might be quicker to get to than Edinburgh but it felt a lot more alien.

Luckily she didn't have to think or organise herself at all; a driver was waiting for her as she stepped out of the bustling, light-filled Gare du Nord station with its imposing Gothic façade and, before she had a chance to take in the fact she was actually in Paris at last, he had pulled away into the heavy traffic.

It was only then that Polly realised she had no idea where the meeting was being held. He could be taking her anywhere. She shuffled through the papers Rachel had handed her, looking for some kind of clue.

Nothing. Budgets, technical specs, nothing of any use.

She felt so helpless, the annoyance itched away at her. The tiredness was bad enough; the effort it was taking to function at her usual level was soul destroying. Clara's reassurances that it wouldn't last, that she would be back to full capacity in just a couple of weeks, were little comfort. She couldn't afford to slack at any point.

Nobody had said it would be easy—and 'nobody' was right—but she couldn't let that derail her. Her grandfather might have apologised but she wasn't going to give him the slightest opportunity to think she couldn't cope.

The car drew up outside an imposing-looking hotel built of the golden stone Polly had already noticed in abundance as they drove down the wide boulevards. Each floor was populated with quaint balconies while colourful flower baskets softened the rather regal effect.

The driver had come around to open her door. *'Mademoiselle?'*

'I'm meeting him here?' she asked, puzzled. Polly knew a five-star hotel when she saw one and this looked top end. This kind of old-world luxury seemed a peculiar choice for a cutting-edge developer. Maybe it was a post-modern thing she wasn't cool enough to understand.

Either way she was here now—and the hotel certainly was Paris at its opulent best. The Eiffel Tower was clearly visible from the pavement and the foyer reminded her a little of Rafferty's with its art-deco-inspired floor and grand pillars. Polly looked around. How was she supposed to work out which particular bar, restaurant or café she was meeting her contact in—and what *was* his name again?

'Can I help you?' The intimidatingly chic receptionist spoke in perfect English. How did she know? Did they have a nationality detector at the door?

'Yes, I am Polly Rafferty and I am supposed...'

'Ah, Mademoiselle Rafferty. I have your key here. There is nothing to sign. It is all taken care of.'

'Key?' Polly took it in her hand. It was a key too, a heavy gold one, not an anonymous card. 'No, I'm not staying. I am meant to be meeting...' She thought hard. Nope. Nothing. Had Rachel ever told her the name? 'Someone,' she finished lamely.

'Yes, I know. Pierre will show you the way.'

It was a bit like being in a Hitchcock plot. Polly fully expected Cary Grant to walk past as the dapper porter showed her to the lift, not betraying by one eyebrow how odd it was for her to be checking in without as much as an overnight bag.

If checking in she was. Maybe he was merely showing her to a meeting room?

The lift went up. And up and up.

'Penthouse?' she queried. It was an odd place for a meeting room. Pierre merely motioned for her to follow and led her to a white door, the only one in a grand, formal-looking corridor richly papered in a gold and black oriental print.

I'm being kidnapped and I am far too English and polite to scream for help, Polly thought as she put the key into the lock and turned it. The door swung open and she found herself looking at quite the most perfect hotel suite she had ever seen.

The door opened into a large sitting room. Polly stepped in, her attention immediately captured by two floor-to-ceiling windows, both flung open and leading out onto one of the pretty balconies she had admired on the way in. Perfectly visible through both was a to-die-for view of the Eiffel Tower, majestically dominating the horizon.

Polly turned slowly, taking in her luxurious surroundings. The suite was decorated in shades of lavender and silver, the cool colours perfectly setting off the rich mahogany tones in the woodwork. Two sofas, lavishly heaped with cushions, surrounded the dark wooden coffee table and lavender silk curtains framed that perfect city view. Polly stepped further in, looking back at Pierre for confirmation, but he had gone, closing the door behind him. She was alone.

If this was a kidnap then it was a luxuriously comfortable kidnapping. Her gaze stopped on a plate on the coffee table. A kidnapping complete with a plate of delicately coloured macaroons.

Polly had never stayed anywhere this beautiful. It wasn't that she couldn't afford to, but, her recent trip aside, she really only travelled for business and that was on Rafferty's budget. She stayed in good hotels, in comfortable, spacious rooms fully outfitted for the business traveller, but she would never charge a suite like this to her expense account.

And it had never occurred to her to book this kind of luxury for herself. What had she been thinking? From now on it was suites all the way.

She wandered around taking in each lavish detail. All the accessories from the light switches to the lamps, the vases to the mirrors, had a nineteen twenties art deco vibe to them. In fact, Polly narrowed her eyes, she was no expert but that fruit bowl looked pretty genuine to her.

If the bathroom had an enormous roll-top bath vast, thick towels and an array of scented crean

and bubbles then Polly had either died and entered
her own personal heaven or was in some kind of
weird reality show tailored to her every need.

She tiptoed through the large bedroom, noting
with approval the terrace off it, complete with sun
loungers, and entered the bathroom.

Oh! It was utterly perfect.

Would it be very wrong to have a bath when she
was supposed to be prepping for the oddest business meeting she had experienced in ten years of
work?

Reality asserted itself. A chill ran through her.

What kind of meeting was this? She should go
back into the sitting room and take advantage of
her solitude to complete the prep work she had
neglected on the way here. More importantly she
should phone Rachel and find out what on earth
was going on.

Maybe, if this was all a mistake, she could book
the suite anyway. After all, she was here now. She
was finally in Paris. It would be a shame to just
turn around and make her way tamely home now
that her mother's spell was broken.

With a last longing glance at the bath Polly returned to the sitting room, resisting the urge to bounce on the bed as she passed it.

It was all just as gorgeous when she walked back into the main room but it just didn't have the same effect. The suite felt too big, too spacious. Too lonely.

This was why she had never stayed anywhere like this. This was a suite made for two. For lovers. From the massive bed to the double tub, the twin sun loungers to the sumptuous robes, it was a place heavy with romantic possibilities.

Polly walked over to the window and out onto the balcony, looking at the Eiffel Tower more like a set from a film than an actual view. What would it be like to be here with someone else? Sipping champagne—or, for her, right now, some kind of fruit cordial—and watching the city below?

What would it be like to stay here with Gabe?

Polly tried to push the thought away but it stuck there, persistent. She had shared so much with him the last few weeks. If only she could share this too. Had she tried hard enough to get through to him? After all, she had pretty much told him that she was giving up and putting the baby first.

Had that been the right thing to do? It had certainly been the sensible thing, the logical thing.

But should she have fought harder?

Her hands clenched. In her desperation to prove that she wasn't her mother, had she thrown away her only chance at happiness?

A soft knock at the door pulled her out of her introspection and she gave the view one last, longing look. It was time to work.

She should have the meeting and then, maybe, she would think again. Make a final decision. Stick with it this time. She couldn't keep second-guessing her choices.

She didn't usually. Maybe this was a sign that she had got it wrong...

Another knock, a little louder this time.

'Yes, I'm coming...' If only she could remember his name!

She was going to have to wing it. Polly walked over to the darkly panelled door and opened it, words of apologetic welcome on her lips.

Only to falter back as she clocked the tall, dark-haired man on the threshold.

'Gabe? Are you in this meeting as well? Thank goodness. I am woefully ill prepared. I can't even remember the developer's name. Although I *will* deny it if you quote me on that.'

Gabe didn't say anything and she continued, the words tumbling out. 'Do you have any idea why he has arranged to meet us in such an odd place? Although it is completely beautiful. You should see it, it's like a slice of heaven. With macaroons *and* views.'

Okay, she was definitely gabbling.

But better gabbling than grabbing him by his lapels and dragging him in close. Better gabbling than flinging her arms around his neck and pressing her lips to his.

But, oh! How she wanted to. Especially now.

Her eyes took him in greedily. It was unfair. No man should look so good. It wasn't as if he were dressed any differently from his usual smart-casual style. Perfectly cut grey trousers, white linen shirt open at the neck, hair falling over his forehead, heavy stubble shadowing his sharply cut jaw. Standard Gabe.

Utterly irresistible.

How could she walk away?

She couldn't. She wouldn't.

She would try again, fight harder. Both she and

the baby needed her to fight. Needed Gabe in their lives.

She stood aside as he strolled into the room. *'Bonjour*, Polly.'

She was going to make him see. If she could only figure out how.

She was biting her lip, looking thoroughly confused. It was kind of adorable seeing Polly off-kilter.

'I spent the last two years here in Paris,' he said, walking over to the window and looking out at the spectacular view.

It was like seeing the city for the first time, seeing it through her eyes. Golden, exciting, full of possibilities.

'I know, you were working at Desmoulins.'

'I had an apartment not far from here. I got up, jogged to work, worked, ate out, met friends, worked out. All in Paris.'

He took a step out onto the balcony and breathed in the city air. Car fumes, cooking smells, the river. It had always choked him before but today it was welcome. Felt fresher somehow.

Polly stood in the room for a moment and then

came out to join him, looking around her in awe. 'It's even more beautiful than I thought it would be. It must have been hard to leave.'

Gabe shrugged. 'Not really. It was just a place. A place to climb up the ladder a little further. It didn't mean more to me than New York or San Francisco.'

'Oh.'

'I was hoping that if I came back to Paris with you, if I walked the streets with you, then that might change.

'I was hoping it would become magical.'

The words hung there. Anxiously Gabe scanned her face but he couldn't read her expression.

'I don't understand,' she said finally. 'Is this a test? If I don't feel the pea through twenty mattresses I'm not a princess and we're not worth fighting for? Is that what you mean?'

'*Non.*' She hadn't understood. His heart speeded up; he could feel it thumping through his chest. 'Polly, you told me to go and like a coward, like a fool, I went.'

He grimaced. 'I told myself it was for the best, that I was doing it for you. But I don't think it can be for the best. I don't think anyone can feel the way I feel about you, love you the way I love you, and not be with you.'

He'd said it. Surely the sun should burn a little brighter, the birds sing louder. Some acknowledgement somewhere that he had finally cracked open his shell.

'I don't understand.' She turned to him, eyes huge and clouded with an emotion he couldn't identify. 'What about the meeting?'

Damn the meeting. What about his words? He'd rushed in, confused her. 'It's not until Monday. I asked Rachel to get you here early so we could have the weekend. The weekend for you to try and see the magic, see if I'm worthy.' He swallowed. Had he misjudged so badly?

'If you want to, that is. Your ticket will let you return today if you would rather, or you can have the room on your own. It's paid for, it's yours...'

He paused, waiting, heart thudding as the seconds passed.

Her voice was small. 'You arranged all this?'

'*Oui*. For you. Although,' he added fairly, 'Rachel helped.'

Her mouth turned up. A smile. It was like a

medal awarding him hope. 'I had no idea. I guess she can be discreet after all.'

'I tried to plan it all. I looked up all the romantic things to do in Paris but they all seem to involve champagne or cocktails, which is no fun for you. And I thought, if we need a list to find the magic then something is wrong. So I tried again.'

'You did?' She took a step closer, the tilt on her mouth more pronounced, a gleam of hope in her eyes.

'I thought, what would Polly like? And I knew.' At least, he hoped he knew. 'Old Paris. Shopping at all the best vintage and antique shops, strolling around Montmartre paying our respects to the artists of the past. The Catacombs.'

It wasn't too exhaustive an itinerary, not for three days. Organised enough for Polly to have a sense of purpose, fluid enough for some spontaneity.

Her mouth trembled. 'What if there isn't any?'

'Any what?'

Her eyes closed briefly, the long lashes sweeping down.

'Any magic?'

Gabe's heart thudded, audibly, painfully. 'Polly,'

he said, taking her hands in his. 'For me there is magic wherever you are. I don't need a walk around old streets to prove that. I can't wait to show Paris to you, can't wait to see you buy out the vintage shops or discover a new café with you, but I don't need to do these things. I just want to do them for you. With you.'

Her hands folded around his. 'Really?' she whispered. 'What about next week, next month, next year?'

He tightened his hold, drawing a caressing finger along her hands. 'I can't tell you I'm not afraid,' he said honestly. 'Your life is changing so quickly and if we do this, mine will too. I didn't want to cause my parents more pain. The thought of putting you through that...' He inhaled, a deep painful breath.

'I got given my life back but somewhere along the way I forgot to live it. It was easier not to care. I thought I was in control. I set goals. I worked, I ran, I didn't stop. The more I worked, the harder I pushed my body, the less I had to think. I thought I had found a way to conquer my demons, a way to take charge, but I was hiding. And then you came along and ripped my hiding place to shreds.'

'I'm sorry.' Tears were trembling on her lashes and he released one of her hands to capture the sparkling drop.

'Don't be. I've been more alive the last few weeks than I was in the last ten years. I worked away this week,' he confessed. 'Stayed at the vineyard, spent time with my parents.' He smiled at her. 'Trying to get my number one spot back with Jean. You're right, of course, there's a lot I can help them with even in England. Advice, contracts, that kind of thing.'

'I'm glad. They're so lovely.'

'That's funny, they say the same about you. I have to admit there's a bit of me that thinks you'll agree just to spend more time with my parents.'

'Agree to what?'

'To marry me.'

Polly blinked. Had she heard him right? 'To what?'

Gabe squeezed her hands tighter. It was almost painful but she was glad of the contact. It was proof that she was actually here, on a balcony in Paris, being proposed to.

'I should be on one knee...'

'No,' she said quickly. 'Just say it again.'

'I don't have a ring. I hoped we might include some jewellers on our antique trail, find something vintage. Sapphires, like your eyes. I was going to wait till then but I can't,' he confessed, the dark eyes so full of love it almost hurt to keep looking into them. 'Polly Rafferty, *je t'aime*. And if you would do me the honour of letting me in, of being my wife, then I promise I will always love you. And the baby. I'll be the best husband, the best father I can be. I want to start living again, Polly. I want to start living with you by my side.'

Polly struggled to find the right words. She couldn't. She had no idea what to say. 'And Mr Simpkins?'

'He has always had my heart,' he assured her, his face lightening with hope, with love. 'Mr Simpkins, Rafferty's, Hopeford. Everything you love, I love too. And I hope you feel the same way about my home, my family. My heart belongs to you.'

'And you have mine.' It wasn't so hard to say the words after all. 'I know the future is utterly terrifying. But with you by my side I can face it, whatever it holds.'

Gabe let go of her hands, reaching up to cup her face, pushing her hair back, his hands tangling themselves in its lengths. 'Are you sure?'

Polly slipped her hands around his waist, pulled him in closer. 'I've never been surer of anything. I love you too, Gabe. I think I loved you from that very first day. I had never met anyone so infuriating, so annoying, so challenging.' She smiled up at him. 'Anyone I fancied more.'

'I thought you were going to slap my face.'

'The accidental kiss? I think it was meant to be.' She stood on her tiptoes and found his mouth at last, cool and firm and sure. 'I think we were meant to be. I think it was magic.'

EPILOGUE

POLLY DIDN'T THINK Rafferty's had ever looked more beautiful. Her talented window dressers had moved some of the make-up counters and beauty areas back, draping the rest in purple and cream fabric, and suspended huge intricate paper sculptures in the same colours from the ceiling. Upstairs, she knew the tearooms were decorated in similar colours ready to welcome her wedding guests.

A stage dominated the middle of the floor, right under the point of the iconic dome. Cream vases, the size of a small child, were filled with silver branches creating an ethereal woodland effect.

The chairs were set in a wide semi-circle around the stage, each row flanked with a massive altar candle, the flames casting a dancing light over the room, discreetly backed up with the store's lowlights.

They were usually open until nine in the evening on a Saturday but today, for her wedding, Rafferty's had done something even the Blitz had never forced them to do.

They had closed early.

Most of the seats were already filled. Suited men and elegantly dressed women in a bright assortment of colours whispered and snapped pictures of the fairy-tale scene. There were several overexcited children fidgeting beside their parents, tugging at their best clothes, and Polly breathed a sigh of relief knowing she had a room put aside for them, complete with films, toys and paid babysitters to watch over the younger guests.

Peeking over the balcony, Polly spotted her grandparents, regal in the front row, entertaining Monsieur and Madame Beaufils. Her heart gave a little squeeze of joy, her family. All together.

'Are you ready?' Clara touched her shoulder softly.

Polly shivered. 'I think so. I didn't expect to be nervous but now that we're here I'm beginning to wish that we'd run away and got married in secret.'

Clara laughed. 'Summer would never have forgiven you. This is her moment of glory. I wouldn't have forgiven you either and nor would Hope. It's not every three-month-old who gets to be a bridesmaid.' She dropped a kiss on her niece's's fuzzy head.

'She looks gorgeous,' Polly agreed, beaming at her small baby who was trying her best to eat the silk sleeve of her cream dress.

'Best dressed girl in the room.'

'For now.' Polly eyed her daughter darkly. 'I have three changes with me. I'm not sure that will be enough.'

'It's a good thing there's a whole baby department just one level up.'

'Clara...' Polly pulled at her skirt, her fingers nervous, '...will I do?'

The other woman smiled. 'You're beautiful,' she said.

Polly inhaled, a long deep breath. Her dress was simple, an ankle-length cream sheath, her loose hair held off her face with a beaded band. It was an utterly simple yet perfectly elegant outfit; a Rafferty's original, copied from one of the old designs Polly had found in the archives.

Clara smoothed down her own purple dress, a loose design that skimmed over her stomach, flattering the bump. There would be less than six months between the cousins and Polly couldn't wait to meet Raff's child. The smaller bridesmaids, Summer and Hope, were looking uncommonly neat and tidy in cream. For now. The chances of them ending the evening in their current outfits were pretty slim. Especially Hope, who was currently averaging four changes a day.

'I don't know.' Polly watched as Hope fiddled with the delicate platinum bangle she had given Clara as a bridesmaid gift. 'You were a pretty gorgeous bride.'

'I was marrying Raff,' Clara said simply, her green eyes glowing with love. 'I would have been happy with a sack and a takeaway.'

Polly grinned, she knew full well that Clara had adored every moment of her winter wedding to Raff. She would have preferred something smaller herself but Gabe wanted the world to see them become a family.

And she could deny him nothing.

They had started adoption proceedings as soon as they could but Gabe couldn't have adored Hope more if he had fathered her, and, Polly thought loyally, he had in every way that mattered—from holding Polly's hand through the long, arduous labour to night feeds and nappy changes.

The assembled guests had been talking quietly but when two tall men made their way to the front the murmuring ceased and heads craned to get a better look at the groom and his best man.

Dressed in identical morning suits, the two men couldn't have looked more different. Although they were of a similar height Raff was built on broad lines, his hair as blond as Polly's own, his brand of good looks deceptively boyish. Gabe was leaner, darker with a more dangerously attractive demeanour.

'They're there,' she told her friend shivering with anticipation as her grandfather climbed the sweeping stairs to join them, pride beaming in his face as he readied himself to escort his granddaughter down the makeshift aisle.

Polly gripped Clara's hand tightly and then took a deep breath, turning to greet her grandfather father with a kiss. She was ready.

Clara was poised, ready to go first, Hope in her arm, then Summer would follow on. Waiting out front, sprinkled throughout the congregation was her grandmother, her parents-in-law to be and all three of Gabe's sisters with assorted husbands and children. Waiting for her at the bottom of the aisle was her brother, tugging at his cravat.

And Gabe. Her fiancé, father of her child. His eyes were fixed on hers, a small, private smile just for her on those well-cut lips.

This time last year she had had no one. Now she was just ten minutes and a few words away from a huge, extended, noisy, chaotic, loving family. A challenging, questioning, adoring, supportive husband. She had a daughter, dependent on her for everything.

There was a time all this would have terrified her. But now?

Polly smiled back at Gabe. 'I love you,' she mouthed.

His sensual mouth curved. *'Je t'aime,'* he mouthed back.

Polly Rafferty was completely and utterly happy.

* * * * *